A Love Supreme

A Love Supreme

A Novel

Kent Nussey

The **Mansfield** Press

National Library of Canada Cataloguing in Publication

Nussey, Kent, 1954-
    A love supreme / Kent Nussey.

ISBN 1-894469-11-9

I. Title.
PS8577.U86L68 2003   C813'.54   C2003-902682-5
PR9199.3.N87L68 2003

Editor: Alexander Scala
Cover and Text design by Tim Hanna
Cover photo courtesy of Nonstock, 2003
CAN YOU HEAR IT TOO? — sculpture by Mitchell Fenton
Photo by Denis De Klerck
Author photo by Barry Munger

The publication of *A Love Supreme* has been generously supported
by The Canada Council for the Arts and
the Ontario Arts Council

Mansfield Press Inc.
25 Mansfield Avenue Toronto, Ontario, Canada M6J 2A9
Publisher Denis De Klerck
www.mansfieldpress.net
Printed in Canada

This book is for Barry Munger and Jay Stapleton

"Thee will I follow far as is allowed me,"

He answered; "and if smoke prevent our seeing,

Hearing shall keep us joined instead thereof."

Dante (Purgatory XVI, 34-36)

Part I

Late in the morning, as Omar sat hunched over his typewriter, the telephone rang. He looked up, uncomprehending, from the page that sprouted from the carriage; the phone chirped again and he turned to stare at it, just out of reach on a small table beneath the window. On the fourth ring he bolted from his chair and snatched up the receiver.

"Yes!" he said.

"Omar? Omar! Hey! It's Megan."

"Megan."

"Hey, I haven't seen you in weeks! I thought of you yesterday when I was crossing Queen Street near my house and this old man got hit by a car — " Megan spoke in a rushed shout that made Omar wince as it funnelled through the receiver. "It was so *weird*! This old guy got slammed by a station wagon and it lifted him about a mile in the air and his raincoat exploded into a shower of coins."

"Coins," Omar said.

"Yeah! His pockets were stuffed with nickels and dimes and they fell all over the street and ran clinking right up to the curb. I picked one up while it was still rolling."

Omar started to speak but she cut him off.

"But before I forget I wanted to tell you that we should hook up for a drink or something before Christmas. I don't know what you're doing for the holidays, but I'll be around — "

Omar glanced at the wide calendar tacked to the far wall. Christmas was exactly one week away. His mind raced ahead, trying to gauge his progress on the book. He'd promised his editor a full draft by the spring, but already he had the sinking feeling that time was running out. His attention jerked back to the noisy voice in his ear. Megan was asking him something.

"Hold it." He made her stop. "Say that again."

"What? You – what?" she gasped, breathlessly annoyed. "Oh – I said Paulette and Duncan said I could bring you to their house on Christmas night, if you're free. I thought you might be and told them we'd come after dinner. They have a huge family dinner on Christmas night and then their friends stop by later on. It's a tradition. Paulette said to come by for drinks around nine or ten."

Megan had regained her momentum and Omar held on, the receiver an inch from his ear.

At last he broke in again: "I should get back to work, Megan. But I'll probably be here Christmas day. More than likely."

"Right," she said tartly. He thought she might be offended, but her voice settled into a casual timbre. "Okay then. I'll tell Paulette we'll come in the evening. They live just down the street from you."

"I can't believe Christmas is next week," he said. "But sure, tell her we'll stop by."

"Great. Well, I'll call you before that. Maybe we can get that drink."

"Sure. Maybe. Give me a call."

She hung up and Omar went back to the metal-bodied typewriter mounted on the large wooden desk like an engine. He studied the page curling out of it, the pen and pencil scrawls in the margins. The curmudgeonly absurdity of the machine both pleased and alarmed him. Six months ago, just before he moved into the second floor of this house, he'd sold his car, his computer, and his fax machine to buy the time he needed to finish his book. For the same reason, and at the same time as his move to this quiet downtown side street, he'd also given up his column with the newspaper and the rest of his freelance contracts. Since then he'd devoted himself to the manuscript, which he'd pitched to his editor as straight-ahead biography of three seminal jazz figures – Monk, Mingus and John Coltrane. But almost immediately, in the Monk section, it had become clear to Omar that he was writing a highly personal response to what he termed "the extra-musical genius" of these legendary musicians; not only a chronicling of their careers, but also an increasingly metaphysical treatment of their quests into the realms of mystery and wonder, realms that were hard to enter by way of mere logic and critical prose.

The abandonment of journalism and the move to a new neighbourhood had been good for the project. On that point he felt certain. But always at the back of his mind lay a specific fear that by trading his car, his electronic accessories and his already irregular income for time and this typewriter, he had left the door open for any number of reversals that might hurl him into the street. Not that his seven-year-old Toyota and his computer had commanded staggering sums, but they had at least possessed symbolic properties that he could cling to when the street loomed nearer.

He sat with his hands on the typewriter's metal flanks as if to steady himself. Even now, he reasoned, he had money in the bank and still owned, beyond his CD system, a turntable and a cache of vintage LPs that gave him comfort and contributed important aural information to his work. Moreover, he possessed two degrees in musicology and journalism was not his last recourse.

And yet he couldn't shake the jittery feeling that his regression in technologies, once begun, might trip some larger mechanism of destiny that would slowly undo first his biographical enterprise, and then him.

Omar sat as if entranced above the darkly gleaming corpus of the typewriter and rebuked himself for breaking his concentration to answer Megan's call. He shook his head and let the frustration float out of him in a massive sigh. The frustration itself he took as a sign that he needed to get out more. After all, Megan was an attractive woman, statuesque and red-headed with a wonky social energy that was sometimes diverting. He should be grateful she'd asked him. It wasn't as if he'd had other plans.

He stood up and peered down through the window to the narrow grey street, the century-old red-brick houses crowded shoulder-to-shoulder like headstones. No, Christmas required some social contact to make it bearable – a few holiday drinks in a real home, with a real family, to make the day pass. Mildly buoyed by the prospect, and vaguely reassured he'd taken several steps away from that threatening dereliction, he hunkered down at the desk again and tapped out a new sentence, and then another, until once more he was riding a jagged rhythm on the sturdy machine.

φ

Hours later, Omar turned off the lamp and leaned back in his chair. The dull afternoon had ripened into a richer, potent darkness in the window near his desk. His body felt tense, but a numb fatigue blanked his brain and the nerves around his eyes. His attention caught on the white and red and green lights strung through the blackness outside. The season touched him with a merely intellectual nostalgia for people and places he could scarcely recollect. But likewise it contained the suggestion of something else, an imminence or an expectation, he couldn't quite put his finger on. Several times in recent weeks, while walking down the busy streets in the blue winter dusk, he'd had a powerful sensation that he'd just passed or was about to pass a long-lost friend from another town, another existence. He recognized the posture of a former teacher in a dignified behatted man paused at a newsstand, or a long-forgotten aunt appeared in the gait of a small bundled-up woman crossing the street in front of him.

Omar turned on the other lamp near the telephone and tapped the numbers to call Harris. He held the receiver to his ear while he stared at the carnival-like lights in the outer darkness. After three rings Harris' voice message came on: *The greatness of man is that none can save him.*

His friend's sepulchral tones, followed by the shrill mechanical beep, made Omar smile, and he remembered that Harris had flown to Costa Rica to do a catalogue for an outdoor clothing company and wouldn't be back until the weekend. Omar hung up without speaking, pressed the redial button, and listened again. Harris was a strikingly handsome eccentric who studied Sufi texts and translated French poetry and modelled on the side to support these preoccupations. He often had a free hour to bike over to Omar's neighbourhood for a quick coffee or beer. His dismissive talk about oddballs in the modelling business could turn on a dime into rambling discourse on obscure Bosnian poets or Nepalese composers. These tidings of the larger world pleased Omar, partly because Harris, despite his lean good looks, was at least as inward and solitary as Omar himself. The glottal pronouncements Harris left on the telephone – an aphorism of Krishnamurti, or of Nietzsche or Camus – scared off the telemarketers and the occasional woman who thought Harris might live up to his literal image, but Omar had come to look forward to these recitations, and he often jotted the current one on the back of an envelope while the recording played.

He hung up a second time and looked out at the night. Who else could he call on such short notice? But after all, why should he feel compelled to seek out company when he knew he'd be perfectly content to unwind with a beer or two by himself? That was all he needed, really. Just a beer or two to decompress. Moving quickly, he turned off the lights, pulled on his overcoat, and jogged down the stairs and out of the house.

He strolled absently down the sidewalk, beside the wet street that reflected coloured lights from the houses. At Dundas he crossed, dashing through the remnant of rush hour, then slowed to a stroll again in the park. As he drifted among the bare trees a burden seemed to lift and for the sheerest instant he thought he heard music. With a sudden and surprised awareness he lifted his eyes, as if summertime hovered between the black branches and the city's miasmic white glow. The feeling vanished and Omar walked on with the fading recognition that what had left him had once been the everyday essence of his life. He breathed the unseasonably mild dampness, held it in his chest, let it go.

The park path took him to a side street, one slightly more well-to-do than his own but not nearly so festive with lights and ornaments. He walked faster until it met Queen Street, where he lingered at the hectic intersection and took in the ordinary spectacle of cars and striding couples and the bright trolley interiors grinding by like old-fashioned diners on wheels. He turned and walked slowly toward the bar, glancing into the cafés and art spaces sandwiched between junk shops and second-hand appliance stores. Two or three years ago this area had been a precinct of hookers and of woebegones from the sprawling mental hospital two blocks west. Then an old factory had been converted into lofts, then two or three roachy lunchrooms had turned into cute brunch spots or small galleries. Nevertheless, the neighbourhood still twitched in the shadow of the mental institution. By daylight its spectral denizens slouched on corners and huddled in doughnut shops. At twilight they wandered back to the vast, prison-like edifice to be fed, medicated and locked in for the night. Last summer, his first in the area, Omar had often walked around the hospital buildings and followed the massive brick wall of the original Victorian asylum that bordered the grounds. He would press his fingers into the wall's gouged and stained surface, the brick so old he could flick it away with his thumbnail. Sometimes, in the hot weather, he'd sat in the wall's otherworldly shadow and watched the fuzzy souls teetering down the manicured walkways or dozing on the benches like tragic statues. Occasionally, like an exclamation in a dream, an albino squirrel would scamper across the lawns behind them. Then Omar would cross the street and walk back to the brand new restaurant-bar with the pristine glass front to sit at the white marble counter, so cool and solid under the air conditioning. He'd sip cold beer to continuous piped jazz and stare out at the baking sidewalk where the hip, the glowingly young, and the conspicuously successful passed obliviously beside the decrepit, the demoralized and the genuinely deranged.

For a moment, here and now, he stood on the sidewalk just outside the bar and raised his face to the mild rain. He listened to the long tapering hiss of the traffic that faded, resumed and faded again. A leather-clad woman gripping a cellphone to her head bumped into him, excused herself with a suave snarl, and hurried on. Omar glanced after her. A trace of perfume hung on the drizzly air. Then he went inside.

The first thing he noticed, as usual, was the music – a kind of lilting detective jazz that never quite succumbed to irony. The broad-chested bartender, polishing a glass behind the counter, looked up and smiled. Omar slid his coat over the back of the high bar-chair. The bartender put down the glass and came over.

"It's been a while," he said in a voice that always surprised Omar for its softness.

"You're right. I'll make up for it tonight."

He asked for a pint of lager and the bartender, a polite weight-lifter from the suburbs, drew it without speaking. A glossy black braid hung like a supple muscle down his back: his tight black shirt and pants set off the hairless white solidity of his face and arms. As he set the tall glass before Omar he spoke in quiet but eager tones about the heavy-duty snow blower he'd just purchased.

"It has front-wheel drive and you have to guide it like a plough horse," he said, raising his thick, sculpted arms and making two fists. "Now all we need is snow."

Omar laced his fingers around the glass and imagined the bartender's orderly winter life: an immaculate strip of asphalt between mountains of blown snow, a pewter-coloured SUV snugged securely in a clean garage. Omar liked the bartender because he spoke haltingly, yet affectionately, of these things; he had no gift of gab, never tried to extend the patter beyond his range. But he talked along with uncomplicated good will and a reticence – a shyness, really – that gave Omar time to shift into social gear. After the long hours at his desk he found it difficult at first to make human sounds and project them into quotidian air. He tipped back the heavy glass and took a long swallow.

"I kind of like it that there's no snow," he offered. "I like being able to see grass and colours still."

The bartender smiled obligingly and went back to polishing the glassware. Often, on weekends, a woman worked with him – an Icelandic blonde with ice-blue eyes and a warm, slippery laugh. Omar didn't see her now. Just as well: she'd push a real conversation and he didn't feel up to that yet.

He took another swallow and looked around.

Down the row of booths against the far wall, several couples held wineglasses and chatted over early dinner. Three seats to his left, a well-dressed elderly man with an imperial goatee and a European air lifted a snifter with a golden spot of brandy on the bottom. His snow-white goatee and wavy hair glowed above a pale blue turtleneck sweater that ended just where his whiskers began. To Omar he looked like a serious composer of lugubrious old-fashioned symphonies, an accomplished Strauss or Bruckner at the twilight of his career. With an abrupt deft motion the man threw back his head and upended the snifter so that Omar saw the liquor slide down the glass like slow amber. In a second dramatic gesture, he brought the glass to the counter and stood up; he pushed a tangle of bills toward the bartender, touched his brow, and headed toward the door. Just as he reached it a pair of ultra-thin, ultra-fashionable Asian women came in, laughing and shaking their hair. The goateed gentleman stepped aside and gave them a courtly nod. The women pushed together giggling and moved down the bar like a gangly two-headed, four-legged animal. The man – minus a topcoat, Omar noticed – pushed through the heavy glass door and vanished into the rain-streaked night.

Omar lifted his glass. He felt as though he'd witnessed a changing of the guard. The carefully construed lighting above the white marble bar shed a honey-gold aura, like a diffusion of the composer's brandy. The newly arrived women went through the inevitable queries about where they might smoke; the subdued bartender caught Omar's eye and once again he felt the warm human connectedness begin to flow through his veins. How long had it been since he'd treated himself to a drink in a public space? He thought back to his moment in the park when he had seemed to hear music. Whatever that moment was, slipping through some crack between prescience and memory, it had once been the way he'd felt nearly all the time. But how long ago, and when did it stop? And why had that moment come only now? Was it a good sign?

It occurred to him that since beginning his book he had stopped thinking about the future.

With high, tinkling laughter the women shed little cashmere jackets, silk scarves, and red leather gloves; they installed themselves at the end of the counter, between Omar and the wall-sized window that fronted the streets. While they chattered and dug their cigarettes out of slim leather pouches, Omar contemplated his longstanding solitude. It wasn't exactly isolation, it definitely wasn't loneliness. Not at all. Whatever it was, his solitude was necessary if he was to accomplish the thing he meant to accomplish.

One of the women grasped the other's slender wrist and laughed a bird-like chirp that gave Omar's heart an exquisite bump.

Yes, he'd been working hard and long without a real break from the routine. But it was so very, very difficult to find a productive groove and stay in it. And the material itself wasn't always cheery. The Monk section, which he'd finished in the fall, had been funny, and mysterious, and a little sad. But now, midway through the Mingus chapter, he was struggling: a murky criminality beneath the man's genius darkened Omar's thesis, and Christmas wasn't exactly a Mingus time of year. The music itself never failed to intrigue him, but he had to focus on its most technical elements to find what belonged in his book.

The eerily familiar voice of a woman singing an almost-remembered ballad sifted down from a speaker suspended in the corner. Omar cocked his ear and squinted. It seemed the very voice of the irretrievable past, like the voice of a woman he'd long known and loved without realizing he'd loved her. Just as the song ended he got it: Nancy Wilson singing "How Glad I Am." It had been popular when he was ten or eleven, a dreamy kid taking long baths on Saturday nights with his transistor radio on the shelf tuned to a distant city and a station that played "sophisticated" music: Sinatra, quasi-jazz instrumentals, Peggy Lee and Vic Damone. All redolent of grown-up pleasures and practices he only knew he knew nothing about. He soaked and brooded and listened to those mysterious records for clues to the world to come, to the way he'd be in it. The music took him up, floated him over the complicated midnight city that glittered with passion and intrigue, a city he might one day inhabit and understand.

One of the Asian women touched his shoulder, apologized, lifted her cigarette for a light. Omar looked at her and smiled, as if she might have heard what he'd heard in the song. He blinked and clapped his hand to his shirt pocket, glanced from side to side and reached over the bar to a wide goblet heaped with red matchboxes. He scratched a wooden match against the box and cupped the yellow-green flame with his free hand. With the cigarette poised in her thin lips the woman leaned toward the light. A sleek black wing of hair fell across her face as her cigarette touched the flame: Omar glimpsed the downcast Oriental eye, the glowing cigarette ember and the pouting mouth, before she jerked her head and blew smoke at the ceiling with a breathy sigh. She repeated her apology for disturbing him and turned away.

For a minute or two he continued to stare at the women, as if he had a question to ask them. He heard one of them say, "When I lived in France there was always some man jerking off in the bushes." His thoughts circled back to his childhood reverie. It was true, he guessed, that those Saturday night baths were the beginning of a career, or at least a chronic condition, of listening. Over the years he'd invested the best of his time and intelligence in this sustained act of attention that, to date, had paid only the scantest of tangible dividends. He asked himself if he'd ever really considered the consequences of this investment. Really faced where it might lead him. Over the years he'd made a series of decisions in favour of taking the time he needed to hear the music properly. Yet when he reviewed those years what he saw most prominently were the people and pastimes and physical comforts he'd forfeited. And he was still doing it, still stripping away whatever came between him and the music. For the first time he felt a thrust of genuine misgiving about having sold his car and his computer. Could a man without these things truly prosper in this world?

The bird-like chatter of the women made him glance over. The way they kissed the filter ends of their cigarettes so they wouldn't ruin their lipstick delighted him – and didn't that count for something? He reminded himself: it wasn't only time he'd bought with these forfeitures, but sights and experiences as well. He'd met great musicians and outstanding personages, names that were famous and others that should have been. He'd seen Eartha Kitt in Vegas, Miles Davis in an old downtown theater in Syracuse, New York. In Montreal he'd heard Jimmy Rushing, Mr. Five-by-Five, and even met him after the show – a wheezing tugboat of a man stuffed into a cheap suit bursting at the seams, and no socks, his brown ankles bulging out of scuffed and split brogans.

But his most prized encounter was on a train he took from New York to Wisconsin in a blizzard, just before Christmas. The snow started as they left Chicago: soon after midnight, in the middle of nowhere, not a light to be seen across the snow-smothered plains, the train broke down. Before it rolled to a stop the cars went black, then a few emergency lights flickered on. After the train had sat there for an hour or so, conductors with flashlights came through to announce there'd be entertainment and free drinks in the lounge car. Omar stumbled forward until he found the lounge, jammed with passengers standing around a baby grand piano, a blazing candelabra perched on a table beside it. Behind the instrument loomed a large black man in a pale cardigan who smiled at the crowd while he knocked out cool easy riffs on "Autumn Leaves." Omar listened for a few minutes and pushed closer. This guy was good. His hands gobbled up keys effortlessly: now and then he made eye contact with Omar and nodded, as if he recognized him from some other snowy night, some other San Francisco or Chicago or Montreal. As he played, two barmen in white jackets moved through the crowd with trays of free beer and cocktails. Omar grabbed a scotch and soda and pushed closer still. Only after someone called out, "Play 'Broadway' Mr. Peterson!" did it click. By candlelight, then, on the stalled and semi-lit train, Oscar played and played, until the power clacked on, the lights came up, and the train lurched and groaned and started rolling again. The passengers applauded madly and cheered while Oscar rose and remarked, "Whew! Just in time. I almost ran out of tunes!" Then he bowed, called out, "Merry Christmas, ladies and gents!" and his entourage surrounded him and led him back to his compartment while the train gathered speed and the whistle screamed and Omar, pressed close to a window, stared out at the vast, silent snows.

The bartender set two martini glasses in front of the women beside him. They laughed, touched glasses, and tasted the rose-coloured elixirs with tentative pink tongues before they actually drank. Omar looked beyond them to the wet-black street spangled with bracelets of red and green lights from store windows or upper apartments in the renovated factory. The doubt struck again in ever-widening ripples: what had he made from this life of listening? This investment in the rain and ether of music, what did he expect from it? For years – decades – he had wrestled with this ether; he'd written two million words about music that seemed to solidify it, to give it tactile presence in the practical realms. But in fact he was walking on water, he was turning into water, conjuring an incarnation from the hopelessly personal and finite essences of hope and faith and intuition, some amalgam of all three he could only call music. He'd convinced himself he was building a career, but instead, unwittingly, he'd cultivated a huge solitude and a profound silence, an ever-thinning identity in the world the music came from.

An extra-long streetcar, jointed like an accordion in the middle, jerked to a slow stop at the intersection. The blank faces in the lit cars stared through the dark space between them and the bar, stared at Omar exactly as he stared at them. For a second he wondered what sort of face they saw. An "interesting" face? Or just tired. Then he realized he was gazing directly into the sorrowful brown eyes of a German shepherd dog seated upright between two indifferent humans in the long seat at the end. The dog held eye contact while the light stayed red. Then, as if it finally recognized Omar, its ears rose to alert points. The light changed and the streetcar moved; the dog's elongated head, like an Egyptian god schooled in the Delta blues, swivelled slowly and its eyes stayed on Omar's as the bright carriage passed into darkness.

The bartender set a fresh pint in front of him and hurried to wait on two more women who'd taken seats a few stools to Omar's left. He didn't remember ordering the second pint. He hadn't seen the women come in. They spilled their cigarette boxes and purses and sunglasses onto the marble counter. Omar looked again: yes, sunglasses, on one of the darkest nights of the year. The women

were his age or older, with expensively coiffed and coloured sil-
ver-blond hair, and close-fitting leather jackets, and arresting eyes:
they shared a general style, as if they'd grown on the same tree. But
unlike the younger women on the other side, these two lit their cigarettes with a casual weary grace that bespoke self-assurance and
chronic boredom. It was wonderful, Omar thought, how the delicate
hoist of a cigarette, a cocked wrist, a calm and suggestive eye could
start the imagination rolling. He glanced from the newcomers to the
soft inner lights in a tall loft window across the street. There, half a
storey above the sidewalk, he saw the wide plasma TV churning like
a bright bit of dream pasted to the domestic darkness. What if he'd
played it straight? What if he'd become a lawyer or surgeon and had
married a woman like one of these comely silver-blondes at the bar?
He had the revelation – which he must have had a hundred times,
though it seemed startling and new – that most people he knew and
observed had geared their lives to the attainment of spouses and living spaces and novel gadgets, and if he could only bring himself to
truly want these things in the way other people wanted them his life
might swerve from the shadows and travel on a rail that would carry
him to the end.

One of the blond women said, "Anyone who calls this a world-
class city hasn't been anywhere."

Omar allowed himself a long look in their direction. The one
nearest him, the one who wasn't speaking, held her cigarette in a
small, manicured hand. The cast of her eye, neither tragic or insou-
ciant, betrayed a sort of secular weathering, a legend of experience
with business and men and loss and mitigating acquisition that she
wore surprisingly well. Her friend asked her something about a
gallery, a showing, and Omar thought, Of course, a gallery owner.
She brought the cigarette to her lips and he noticed the finest web-
work of wrinkles around her mouth. The bartender set two stem-
med glasses of white wine before them. Like the younger women,
they touched glasses and sipped. There's no end of it, Omar considered. No end of deals and martinis, cigarettes and wine and veiled

desire like their lidded eyes, and all of it sailing away a little to one side of him, just beyond his reach, his ken, his own obscure need....

A cellphone twittered and one of the Asian women skipped outside to take the call. His eyes followed her, shifted to the loft again and the bright blipping shapes on the TV screen. He saw a partial figure bathed in the uncanny light; perhaps someone lay on a leather sofa across the room. He looked back to the woman huddled near the broad window as she hugged herself with stick-thin arms and spoke into her raised palm. How brittle and how utterly indifferent to her frailty she seemed, framed in the long dark glass.

The music changed to a calypso version of "Mack the Knife" and Omar laughed out loud. The blond woman with the provocatively weary eyes glanced at him. He smiled and looked away. He felt on the verge of remembering something important from his past life, something that might or might not relate to the music. The small, bird-like woman hurried back into the bar with tiny, scuffling steps. The music changed again and for a moment it sounded like the music he'd heard in the park. But the notes were behind the notes he actually heard, like a glass-bead curtain behind a glass-bead curtain. He looked from the black gleaming street to the animated Asian women chattering on his right hand, the svelte worldly blondes to his left; his doubt vanished and instead he felt high, he was getting glorious on the music and faces and he looked back to the street and caught a new face in the window. This time the face knew him and contorted in mock astonishment as she brought up her hand.

"Megan," he said, the glory fleeing out the door as the tall redheaded woman came through it.

"Hey! I thought that was you!" She breathed heavily, as if she'd been walking fast. "I'm on my way to a Christmas party down at the Film Board. I told you about the project I'm working on there — "

She pulled off a long scarf and gave her thick hair a toss; Omar felt the faintest shower of moisture on his face. He looked up and down the bar and saw the place was crowded now.

"Oh my God! What a night! I've been running all over the place."

She threw her coat over the tall chair and ordered a pint of stout.

"Why running — " he started to ask.

"I didn't think I'd see you until next week!" She grinned and brought her face close to his, peering, the pale blue irises of her eyes swimming furiously in dabs of manic light. "I called Paulette about Christmas night and she's expecting us. They'll have a house full of people. You knew that Duncan's mother and sister live downstairs."

Omar said he thought he'd seen the grandmother and the little kids on the streets back in the fall, but he wasn't sure.

"It's so funny you ended up living so close to them. Paulette's been my best friend for ages. Just like you're my best guy friend."

The broad-shouldered barkeep set a darkly foaming glass before her.

"Now that's a pint!" She bumped the full glass against Omar's and slurped some down. "God, I needed that. So how are you? How's the book going? I haven't seen your column lately."

Omar admitted that he'd dropped his newspaper work.

"Really? Wow! That's a leap of faith. They paid pretty well for the column, didn't they?"

"Not bad. But I need more time for the book."

Megan nodded. "I understand that," she said, blandly. "If I was living your lifestyle at your age I'd take a gamble too."

Omar looked at her.

"No, I mean I can see it's time for you to tackle something bigger. Something that will make a splash, for a change. It's now or never, right?"

Omar asked the bartender for a coffee. Whatever revelation or insight he'd felt close to a few minutes ago had vanished, and he wanted to keep his head clear for work in the morning.

"But you must be getting some royalties from the last book, right?" She laughed loudly. "I told my mother you'd published a history of Catholic liturgical music in New Orleans and she thought I was joking."

Omar emptied the cup of black coffee in two gulps and set it on the white saucer. Cups and saucers pleased him in a way he refused to feel apologetic about at this point in his life.

"A lot of people thought that book was a joke," he said.

"Well, I told my mother it must be very readable. I confess I never saw a copy in the store, but I promise I'll order one someday."

"Every bit helps."

"And I always read your columns back then. That four-part piece you wrote about the soundtrack to *Spartacus* – fantastic! I loved it."

Omar smiled dismally. This wasn't a line of talk he wanted to pursue right now. Somehow, Megan felt like bad luck. Not just to herself and the circumstances he'd encounter in her company, but also to his work, to his very imagination. He hadn't thought of it before, and the intensity of his reaction surprised him.

"In many ways you and I are so alike, Omar."

"Think so?"

"Sure. We're both freelancers. We're both into all kinds of music. Music is important to us. The big difference is that I have options."

Startled, he glanced from the corner of his eye and caught her look of somber satisfaction.

"I mean, it's only natural," she said. "It just makes sense, considering how long and hard I've worked to make a name. And let's face it, certain doors open for me."

"The way of the world," he said.

She nodded. "Exactly. That's it. The way of the world."

It's true, he thought, that a smart, handsome woman need never be alone or unemployed in this town.

"Anyhow," she went on, "I'm sure you can get your column back if you need to. It was unique, to say the least."

He emptied the coffee dregs from his cup. "No, I don't think so. I think I burned my bridges at the newspaper."

She gazed at the tiers of shining bottles that lined the wall behind the bar, as if trying to decide on a new drink.

She said, "You know, I'm tight with a couple magazine of editors who might be interested in starting up an Omar Snow column. No, really, your name isn't totally unknown and you need to capitalize on that before it goes cold. You should get on it. Soon."

He stared at her, surprised at the change in her tone. For the first time he noticed her party clothes, the little black cutaway top she wore and the silver necklace that snaked over the powdered and lightly freckled flesh of her collarbone. Not so long ago she'd sported longer hair and funky second-hand jackets and jeans. But now, apparently, she was striving for a more adult and womanly mode. In her mid-thirties, Megan undoubtedly contended with pressures and expectations that Omar, as a semi-employed musicologist, might not wholly understand. For an instant, as he studied her bright and unsound eyes, he nearly felt sorry for her.

"And how's *your* project going?"

She lit a cigarette with her long pale hands and blew smoke toward him.

"The documentary? It's going really well. I think it could turn into something permanent for me, with a little luck. Donnie Mack is a great director. Temperamental, but really talented. He likes me, I think."

She hesitated.

"Did I tell you about this guy I'm seeing?"

"The bouncer?"

"Oh God, no! That's history. I'm really done with younger men. No, this guy's a musician, very sweet, almost my age. His name is Lance. He plays in this neo-psych band that's getting good notices. You'd like him. Hey, maybe we can all get together on New Year's?"

"Why don't you bring him to Paulette's on Christmas?"

"Oh," she said, her voice flattening, "he has to go out of town. His friends always go skiing over the holiday and he promised to go with them. It's a tradition they have."

She drew on her cigarette and lifted her empty glass to get the bartender's attention.

"I'll have one more of these before I leave."

The bartender refilled Omar's coffee cup and brought Megan another glass of stout. The talkative woman who usually worked weekends had come on duty. She waved at Omar from the far end of the bar. As he sipped his coffee he reflected that most of his acquaintances were bartenders or store clerks or waitresses, people he spoke a few words to once or twice a week.

Megan said, "This is maybe the second or third Christmas in my life I haven't been with my family." She paused. "I know you've been alone since your mother died. How long's it been?"

"Couple of years."

"The holidays must be tough."

He shrugged. "Not so much, anymore." But it struck him suddenly as amazing that his family was gone, that the places he'd thought of as home no longer existed in his heart.

"In the spring I'm going to visit my brother in Vancouver," Megan said, and she swung into a rambling digression about brothers and parents and grandparents that tempted Omar's mind to drift. With conscious effort he forced it back and told the bartender he'd have another beer, after all.

The friendly blond woman brought it, placed the glass before him with both hands, and said, "Poor man's speedball."

"What is?" Megan asked.

"Switching back and forth from coffee to beer."

"I know," said Omar. "It'll ruin me."

Once more he tapped his glass against Megan's, and they drank.

Megan asked him, "How do you know the bartender? I mean the woman."

"How? Just from coming in time to time. She talks more than the big guy. She's studying aromatherapy or something."

Again he noticed Megan's partially exposed shoulder under the mellow light, the way her earrings glinted just below her red-gold hair. Yes, she'd definitely altered her style.

"It's hard to think of you as being a regular in a place like this."

"It is? How's that?"

"I don't know. It's easier to think of you drinking Ripple in an empty boxcar or something."

He stared at her and she pushed her head into his chest and made a cooing sound.

"I didn't mean it like that," she said, leaning back, laughing. Then: "You know that Art Pepper book you gave me? I've been dipping into it lately. Now that's the kind of book you ought to write. It's almost frightening because the reader is tapped into his head. You can't escape it. I thought that if you could write a music book like that you'd have a hit."

"A hit."

But he knew what she meant. In fact, she'd put her finger on something that had been nagging him about his own manuscript.

Megan tipped her glass to her mouth and he stole another look at her white neck and her square shoulders that glowed in the soft bar-light. Once, just once, she'd met his pal Harris and they'd promptly taken a dislike to each other. But other male friends would ask him, "Who was that good-looking redhead I saw you with?" And he'd puzzled for a moment, unable to place the person they'd described.

She was telling him about Donnie Mack, the filmmaker she worked for, when Omar interrupted by raising his finger.

"What's this music?"

Megan jerked and straightened: they listened to the stripped-down beat of robotic bass and drums.

"This gets played everywhere now," she said. "It's like a soundtrack that everyone accepts as hip. A safe bet for the management."

Omar listened a moment longer.

"Interesting," he said. "Like the audio equivalent of surveillance cameras. It's cold, but there's a sexy objectivity that's hard to resist."

Megan laughed explosively and he felt it pierce his eardrum like a pointed object.

"Oh man," she cried, "that's what I loved about your columns! You have all these sounds and songs swimming around in your head. You need to get them out in the air." She waved her hand at a cloud of invisible notes swarming above their heads.

Omar smiled and nodded and waited for the music to change.

φ

Outside, as they stood near the broad front window, Megan slipped her arm under his and squeezed close.

"I'll walk to the light with you and get a cab," she said. "God, I'm so late. How many drinks did we have?"

The rain had stopped but the sidewalks were still wet and the street shone black under the lights. She clung to him until they reached the intersection. Immediately a taxi pulled to the curb beside them.

She turned her face and pressed her mouth to his.

"Don't forget about Christmas!" she called as she climbed into the back seat of the car.

Omar watched it swerve fishily back into traffic and tasted the booze-cigarette-perfume taint on his mouth. Just in front of him, a bedraggled hooker got into a salmon-coloured SUV. With his head down, he walked unsteadily toward home. He couldn't explain it, but the encounter with Megan had left him feeling a little bewildered, a little angry. As he turned down the sidestreet that bordered the park he thought about the confusion and dissatisfaction that shone through her fever-bright eyes.

A sudden pain crimped his chest. He stopped on the wet sidewalk and looked up into the gloamy near distance, up to the odd

contraption mounted like a water tower on top of the brick building across the street. Someone – possibly Megan – had pointed
out the device he now stared at, but it was as if he was seeing it
for the first time. He beheld it as a huge Cubist cephalopod, a silver coil the size of a space capsule with a flaring squared bell that
contained a peculiar orange glow beneath the miasmic winter sky.
He seemed to remember someone explaining how the device func-
tioned as a cosmic eardrum, pulling in city sounds and exhaling
them again throughout the building – an artists' co-operative of
living spaces and studios – in a vague tidal roar. But to Omar,
catching his breath, the object might instead have been a fantastic
horn spraying music into the sky over the city, and for a moment, as
the pain in his chest subsided, he envisioned a musician, more like
an angel from Revelation than a man, putting lips to the tapered
end of the horn and blowing stars and planets and suns into the
heavens. Omar stared at it. Was it an eardrum or a horn? Trans-
mitter or receiver? Or, like a great seashell, was it both? Like a great
shell it was both a fossil and a symbol, a figure of Deep Time that
transcended time by drawing in raw temporal sound and spinning
out the fearful music of the spheres. Strange it would strike him
that way just now....

Omar breathed slowly until his head felt clear; then he started
walking again. As he entered the cavernous park he scolded himself for mixing alcohol and caffeine, for wasting time. Plain facts
assailed him: he wasn't young, the current book was a gamble,
and he might run out of funds before he finished it. If he could
just get through the Mingus section and move on to Coltrane. If
nothing else, the writing might be an excuse to listen to all that
gorgeous, exasperating music again. Surely Coltrane's music still
had things to teach him. With luck, he'd get to it in a few weeks.

He took in the dream-like landscape around him. The park was
deserted, dankly cold, and the old-fashioned globe lamps scattered foggy suggestions of ghosts and Victorian murder through
the shadows. He looked over his shoulder and thought about the

mysterious orange glow in the bell of the celestial horn. Tomorrow, he vowed, he'd work extra hard and make up for lost time.

φ

The short days of the following week passed in spasms of intense work at odd hours, often in the early morning, sometimes late at night. But whenever Omar looked out his window the day seemed to be ending, the coloured Christmas lights coming on up and down his street. He left his house infrequently and noted the season with an impatience for the old year to end; it had been a year of burning bridges, and he felt an urgent desire for some new element. He had no clear picture of that element, other than the completion of his book, but more than once, when he stopped typing or put down his pen in the middle of the night, he felt as if he had forgotten something. He would look around his study as if there were some chore or detail he'd overlooked, as if to lay his hand on some appliance that needed fixing, some letter he had neglected to answer.

Three days before Christmas, the snow started. It fell all afternoon and into the night. Just after midnight Omar turned off the lights in his apartment and gazed out at the sinuous sheets of white that filled his neighbourhood. Staring out, he felt a dry rasp of grief for the ending year with all its outward changes and hard work. His mind inventoried the year's gains and losses, setting one against another, adding and cancelling until the exercise fatigued him. When he got down to it, he honestly couldn't say whether it had been a good year – good in the sense of, say, someone like Megan's reckoning of earthly affairs. In any case, he felt relief at its passing.

φ

As promised, Megan telephoned him shortly after noon on Christmas day. She'd spent the morning with an older couple who lived on the first floor of her house, and she was about to go to another friend's house for dinner.

"But I'll stop for you this evening at eight and we'll walk down to Paulette's. She phoned earlier and they're expecting us. You'll like her family and you really should meet them since they're your neighbours, almost."

Omar said he'd be ready and hung up. When Megan phoned he'd been at his desk looking at pages he'd written the day before. He'd bought himself some extra-special coffee and chocolate to celebrate the holiday, but by mid-morning he'd let his eye fall on a page, and before he knew it he'd been drawn back in. Outside, the day was bright and brittle-cold. The tenants above and below him had vacated the house to spend Christmas elsewhere, and as he stood near his desk he felt the pervasive silence, a silence that began in the frigid brilliance above the house and went down to the roots of its foundation. Perhaps someone would call him – some long-lost cousin who recollected the kindness of his parents, or a university friend he hadn't seen in ages. It struck him as extraordinary, even fantastic, that he'd gotten out of bed this morning so totally disconnected from the world of families and friends and domestic rituals. And yet there was another world, just as real and probably more final, and over this last year it had become his intimate. He swore that he sensed it in the creaking silence of this old and empty house.

He turned off the lamp over his desk and went out to the kitchen to reheat the coffee. On the radio he located Handel's *Messiah* and stood listening to the triumphant oratorio as the coffee gurgled and steamed in its small carafe. What was the legend of its composition? That Handel had locked himself in his room with a ham sandwich and dashed off the music in three days. Something like that. But what had been in the man's heart? And how had he matched it so perfectly to the formal elements in his head?

Omar stood absolutely still and listened until the smell of hot coffee reached him. Then he switched off the radio and took his coffee to the main room; he flopped on the couch and stared at the shining, frosted window. How would he spend the rest of the day? Books? Records? A long walk through the deserted streets, he knew, would only depress him. For days he'd been listening to the galloping rhythms of Charles Mingus, but the bit of Handel just now had put a new idea in his head and he wished, for his own good, that the Mingus section were behind him. As he thought about it, and the Monk chapter before it, his confidence faltered: the substance of those chapters and his angle of approach had been shrewd and solid, for sure, but the chapter devoted to Coltrane would test him on all levels. He'd read all the biographies and studies of the musician, and for his money none of them captured the terrible beauty of the music or explained how it related to the self-effacing goodness of the man. How could such things be explained? Omar feared and anticipated the challenge. He knew it would require all his talent and intelligence, and beyond them, prose that was supple and lucid, grounded in the real yet capable of soaring, of turning itself inside-out in order to touch the most ephemeral of human moments. In short, a prose not unlike Coltrane's music, words that clustered like notes and touched all the highs and lows without losing sense. But what was that music? And what made him think he was capable of it?

Looking up, he realized the winter light had bled from the icy windowpane; the cold rooms swarmed with shadows. He should get up, do something, make supper. At that moment the furnace in the basement chugged on, and a stale warmth rolled out from the vent in the opposite wall. Omar closed his eyes, glad of the dark. Restful and solid, dependable as time itself, the dark was the colour of his solitude. He hugged it to himself and told himself he might as well sleep. When he awoke there'd be somewhere to go, people all around him, and the day would have its proper end.

A few minutes after eight his door buzzer squawked and Omar ran down the stairs with one arm in his leather jacket. On the porch Megan stood grinning in an immense overcoat, her fuzzy hat jammed down to her eyes.

"It's brutal out here!" she cried and with stiff, old-ladyish movements she started down the steps toward the street.

Omar pulled his scarf to his chin and zipped his jacket. The cold brought tears to his eyes. Paulette's house was on his street, but he should have brought a hat and gloves.

"If I slipped I'd shatter into a million pieces!" Megan shouted.

They walked quickly, a little unsteadily on the unshovelled sidewalk. Despite the cold, Omar felt his spirits lift as they passed the squat brick houses huddled in a row, their porches outlined in red and green lights or with nets of tiny white bulbs. And above the houses and naked trees, a scattering of frozen stars rode in the clear black sky. Megan waited for him to catch up, then clutched his arm like they were a regular couple on a Christmas date.

"You'll like the Coulters," she said, teeth chattering. "Paulette and Duncan and the kids live upstairs. Louise – that's Duncan's mom – lives on the main floor and Carrie lives in the basement. She worked in New York for six or seven years trying to make it as an actor. A couple of years ago she came back and never moved out. It's an interesting household."

"I guess it would be good to know someone on my street," Omar said.

"They'll like you. You're their kind."

As he considered this she said "Here!" and steered him left, then up several steps to the narrow walkway to the house.

The porch light shone on the white snow, and through the single front window Omar saw into a room of well-dressed people and lit candles on a mantelpiece. He followed Megan up the porch steps. She pressed the bell. Sounds of laughter and music carried dimly on the frigid air. The inner door swung inward, the glass door opened. A woman in a semi-formal dress stood before them, staring out imperiously, as if waiting for them to state their business.

For a second Omar thought that Megan had turned in at the wrong house. But then the woman in the doorway blinked and cocked her head and said, "Oh! It's you, is it? Well come in, come in." She stepped back and motioned. "We've just finished dinner."

Megan stamped her feet and laughed and Omar followed her inside. As he brushed past the other woman he felt her gaze, which was not entirely welcoming, and noted the regal lift of her chin. She was another redhead, and, he realized under the hall light, quite lovely. Megan said Carrie's name and introduced him.

"Right," Carrie said, still watching him. Her eyes were catlike and dispassionate. They seemed to peer at him flatly from prior experience with him or some aspect of him. "I've seen you on the street."

She took his coat and he followed Megan into the noise and warmth of the main room. More introductions were made and Omar shook several hands. He felt off-balance and absurd; surprised, he realized something had flustered him. Megan knew, or had heard of, most of the guests and recited to each the circumstances of their first meeting or the name of the acquaintance they held in common. Carrie reappeared and put a glass of wine in Omar's hand. He realized that everyone in the room was half-sozzled, in a cheery Yuletide sort of way.

Catching his smile, Carrie pressed her hand to the bosom of her dark burgundy dress and declared, "I'm afraid you find us all covered in sin."

Omar laughed a witless sound and she walked off without looking at him.

"Hey pal," Megan said, latching onto his elbow again. "I want you to meet Paulette and Duncan."

She led him to the second floor where a crowd of younger people sat smoking on short black-leather sofas or stood about the punch bowl set on a table still littered with dinner plates. A slim, French-looking woman approached Megan; they laughed brightly, embraced, and Megan introduced Omar to Paulette.

"I've seen you walking by the house," she said. Then, turning to Megan again: "You should have seen dinner. We ran out of food. I told Duncan there wouldn't be enough."

"Where is he?"

"Just over there. Come on — " and she led Omar and Megan across the room.

A tall man in a black blazer turned when Paulette spoke: he looked from Megan to Omar with drink-swollen eyes, but then he shook Omar's hand warmly.

"Glad you could make it," he said. "How's your drink? Plenty to drink — "

He reminded Omar of someone. His style and speech more than his face.

"I hear you're a musician," Duncan said. "What do you play?"

Hard to believe this was Carrie's brother. A different energy entirely.

"No, I just write about it."

"Write about it?"

Paulette said, "Before he went into sales, Duncan played in a pretty good little band. He's really a rock and roll guy."

"I'm really a rock and roll guy," Duncan said, cheerful self-mockery in his voice. He smiled broadly and offered Paulette and Megan cigarettes from his pack. A rounded gold lighter came out of his pocket: Paulette lifted her small hand and Duncan lit the cigarette with a swift, courtly gesture. Something between them, something Omar hadn't been near for a long time, made him want to stand there while they smoked and spoke of the comings and goings of their guests.

"Where's Carrie?" Duncan asked.

Paulette shrugged. "Downstairs. I forgot to tell her Megan was coming."

Megan lifted her orange eyebrows. Drink in hand, Duncan watched Paulette.

"What's that look? What's the difference?"

Duncan blew smoke and reached toward the ashtray on the table.

"Omar hasn't met Louise yet," Megan said quickly, as if eager to change the subject. "There she is. Follow me."

She squeezed Omar's elbow and maneuvered him back toward the punch bowl. He had two drinks in him now and he began to enjoy being led around.

They stopped before a svelte little white-haired woman dressed in red, a strand of pearls around her neck.

"Louise," Megan said, and the woman peered up at them through narrow glasses perched on the end of her nose. "This is my oldest and dearest friend, Omar Snow."

Omar glanced at Megan – he hadn't expected the "oldest and dearest" – and lifted his hand toward the white-haired woman, but her hands were occupied, one with a cigarette, one with a glass of wine.

"How do you do?" she drawled slowly and formally, tilting her head to peer at him more exactly through her spectacles. "So you're the man down the street."

Omar thought he had seen her once or twice on College Street. Obviously she'd been a great beauty in her day, and he was startled to sense something like an alert sexual aura beneath her boozy smokiness.

"I've seen your column in the paper," she said.

"He doesn't do that anymore," Megan told her.

"Oh no?"

"No," he said. "I gave it up."

She squinted over her glasses at him. "My late husband was a journalist. He wrote book reviews, drama reviews, everything."

"Louise worked as a producer at the CBC for years," Megan said. "She's famous there."

Louise sniffed. "That was the old CBC." She blew smoke over her shoulder. "Have you ever done radio, Omar? You have an unusual voice."

He'd been thinking the same about hers, that it reminded him of starlets from the Forties who played shrewd but appealing newspaperwomen or set designers.

"I've always wanted to write," she said. "If I started over again I think I'd write plays and stories for radio."

Her voice was so familiar, so cinematic. Who was it? Bette Davis? Barbara Stanwyck?

"I'm not that kind of writer," Omar said.

A small commotion made them look to the other side of the room.

Carrie waited for everyone's attention. With her hands folded on a violin and a small, tight smile on her face she said, "We've reached the musical portion of the evening. My niece, Ivy, will accompany me on the piano for two or three carols." She spoke in clear, resonant, but slightly aching tones. "And then, if you'd like, we can all sing a few together."

A murmur swept the room as a pretty, wide-eyed girl of nine or ten seated herself at the piano. She fussed nervously, smoothing her skirt and adjusting the bench. She said something in a small, piping voice and everyone laughed. Carrie stood just behind her, tuning her violin. Then she fit it between her shoulder and the curve of her jaw. Her fingers straddled the instrument's neck suavely, competently.

"Ready?" she asked her niece. "Any time...."

And ever so softly, ever so tentatively, the girl picked out the opening notes of "Silent Night." With one or two stumbles they strolled through the carol. At the finish, everyone applauded and the girl tossed her hair and blushed. Carrie counted off the time and they launched into "We Three Kings." Her niece played in a halting, ethereal tinkle; Carrie coaxed her along with clear and fluid strains while Omar daydreamed vaguely of other Christmases with his own family, so very different, so oddly similar to this family occasion. He listened and recollected a Roland Kirk version of the same carol on an album called "We Free Kings," an album he must still own, somewhere, boxed up in a garage or storage locker.

More applause, more laughter.

"What next?" Carrie asked. Her colour was high, and she spoke with a happy breathlessness Omar hadn't heard before.

Ivy shrugged and raised her long, plant-like arms and admitted she didn't know any more carols from the book.

Someone behind Omar called out, "I'll take over!" and Megan darted forward. Ivy scarcely had time to move before Megan took her place on the bench. Carrie shot her a blank stare while she flipped through the book and flattened it open with one hand.

"Do you know this one?" Megan asked Carrie without looking at her. "Okay, here we go! 'Hark, the Herald Angels!'"

Her hands fell on the keyboard and pounded out the familiar chords. Carrie, a little late, tried to match the tempo. They rushed through two more carols in that way, with Megan banging out big chords a beat or two ahead of Carrie, until Carrie suggested "Oh Come All Ye Faithful" and invited everyone to sing.

At the end of one verse, she let the violin drop from her chin and raised the hand that held the bow.

"I think that's enough," she said. "I think Mom has some treats ready for us downstairs."

Scattered applause. People milled about, the younger upstairs smokers mingling with the older well-dressed drinkers from below.

All in all, thought Omar, a civilized occasion, and the music and singing made him feel grateful he'd been invited. He looked around at the flickering candles, the evergreen trim and the sparkling tree. He heard a tipsy guffaw from Louise downstairs, a sound entirely appropriate to the evening. Omar imagined a letter to a friend in which he wrote, "On Christmas night I went out in society for the first time in ages" – as if he were an ostracized bankrupt from some long gone gilded era.

The thing he was, he guessed, was half drunk. If nothing else, the Coulters were expansive hosts, constantly refilling his glass and asking how he liked the neighbourhood.

At that moment Paulette appeared at his shoulder, smiling.

"Are you having a good time? Have you met everyone?"

Omar made himself focus on her dark, sharp-featured face, her boyish grin.

"Wonderful," he said. "This is really great. I can't tell you – I mean, this means a lot to me."

"Oh, don't mention it." Paulette spoke quickly: "We do this every Christmas. We know lots of people who have no family nearby, and it gives Louise an opportunity to visit with old friends she doesn't see all year."

Something caught her eye and she called out, "Tyler! Come here! I want you to meet our new neighbour."

Omar scanned the room, then found himself looking down at a tiny fair-haired boy who gawked up at him with bright, inquisitive eyes.

"Tyler," Paulette began, resting her hands on her son's shoulders, "this is Omar Snow. He lives down the street from us. You'll probably see him around."

The boy's eyes stayed on Omar's as he lifted a small hand. Omar shook it.

"Pleased to meet you, Tyler."

"Hello," he said, still staring up. Then, turning to his mother, "Can I watch a video in my room?"

"Let's get you into bed first and then we'll decide." She looked at Omar: "Everyone's going downstairs for brandy and dessert. Louise has a bottle or two of the good stuff. I'll be down as soon as I get this guy settled in for the night."

With her hands still on the boy's shoulders she pushed him ahead of her toward his bedroom. Omar closed his eyes and tried to remember something. Something important he must not forget. Something about his book. He tried to visualize the stacked and scattered pages that waited for him in the cold dark room down the street. He should get back to them. There was only so much time, so much patience and strength and cash.

When he opened his eyes he was looking at Carrie across the room, just as she accepted a light from a man in a black turtleneck and brown suede trousers. Her cigarette touched the flame from the silver lighter: she exhaled a high plume of smoke and held her cigarette at shoulder level. The way it rested lightly between her fingers and thumb made Omar think of the women in the bar last week. While he watched, Megan approached Carrie and laid her hand on her wrist.

"That was such a gas!" Megan said. "You play so well! We should get together sometime for duets."

Carrie lifted her ethereal cigarette and fixed a cool, level gaze on her: for an instant Omar saw them as through an idealized lens – two comely redheads vying for the world's rarest attentions, two almost-young women with similar expectations; both nearing an age when the brightest options fall away, one by one. Somewhere beneath their minds the first dim alarms had probably rung.

From across the room Duncan called, "When you're ready, come downstairs for dessert everyone."

Megan turned away from Carrie and followed the others. Then, as if snapping out of a strange and persuasive dream, Omar put down his empty glass and trailed after them to the first floor.

φ

By midnight the drinking had gone into high gear; the older guests had left and Duncan had gone back upstairs with two or three of his friends to smoke cigars. Omar found himself settled beside Louise in a small Victorian sofa. Carrie's mother smoked steadily; every now and then she asked Omar to freshen her glass from the dimpled brandy bottle on the mantel. He'd had a few brandies himself and the cozy, Christmasy living room, full of laughter and perfume and cigarette smoke, was exactly where he wanted to be. He looked around and realized he was the only man in the room. This was what he needed. Once upon a time, this had been the life he'd craved. Why? Because he had a talent for it. A talent for laughing and making people laugh and appreciating what it was all about. Minutes ago, Megan had gone out of her way to advertise his bona fides, telling these women that he had written books and published in national magazines. Even drunk, he'd felt their interest quicken, eyes flashing the swift but penetrating second regard. He absorbed it all thirstily and sank deeper in the sofa, happily stunned.

Beside him, Louise reminisced about her youth in Halifax during World War II.

"Everywhere you looked there were men in uniform," she said, slurring her words a little. "My mother wouldn't let me out of the house half the time. I'm telling you, for a teenaged girl it was terribly exciting. Scary, but exciting...."

She leaned toward the massive glass ashtray on the coffee table to tap her cigarette. Omar looked at her dress and thought he had never seen one quite so red.

"We used to sit on this hill that overlooked the harbour," she said, grimacing now and lowering her eyes as if trying to recollect someone's name or face from that vanished life. "Anyhow, that's where everyone went with their boyfriends before they shipped out. I'd never seen anything like it. Couples fucked with abandon in broad daylight."

The younger women smoked and grinned. Louise passed her lipstick-smeared snifter to Omar and said, "Fill Grandma's glass."

Finally Megan broke in to start a convoluted story about her aunt, who had done some amateur theater in the city in the Fifties. Omar thought the story would be about the theater, or the Fifties, but Megan dwelled on her aunt's resoundingly ordinary life in later years, the predictable travels with her predictable husband, the clockwork birthing of three wholesome children. He waited for the climax, the punch line, but none came. Megan rattled on while the phrase *fucked with abandon* repeated itself in Omar's head. Louise stared at Megan over her glasses, her mouth ajar. And just when Omar thought he could take no more, Carrie cried out, "Oh my God! We're out of liquor!" and everyone jumped. Carrie sprang from her chair and bustled into the kitchen. Cupboard doors banged and she returned with a new bottle of brandy, a lit cigarette in her mouth.

"Okay ladies," she said grimly, as she spilled some into each glass, "this is the last bottle in the house. Everybody drink up."

Louise raised her snifter and laughed.

"In the words of Julius Caesar, 'That's all there is and there ain't any more!'"

Megan, rather than minding the interruption, thrust her glass toward the bottle and declared "Looks like I'm in for the long haul."

Omar checked his watch and his equilibrium. One more drink and he'd lose the next two days. He was out of practice, for certain. Now was the time to leave. But a woman named Heather, in reply to a casual question, began to describe her on-line business selling hot glue products. This subject struck Omar as infinitely interesting and he listened until he realized he no longer knew what they were talking about. He looked from face to face, delighted. Such lovely faces. Such beautiful women. He rose uncertainly and said he really must go. A few voices implored him to linger. He shook his head. "It's now or never," he said. While Louise rummaged for his scarf and jacket, the women – all sprawled in sofas and armchairs – bade him goodnight and Merry Christmas and smiled in ways that made him guess the conversation would shift radically the instant he left them.

Louise handed him his things.

"It was very nice to meet you." She shook his hand with surprising firmness while her other hand managed her drink and cigarette.

He thanked her and called a final goodnight over his shoulder into the smoky yellow glow of the living room.

"Goodnight Omar!" the women called back, almost in unison.

Carrie saw him to the door, playing her role as hostess. As he fumbled with his scarf, she said, "Thank you for coming. I hope you don't regret it in the morning." She looked relaxed and completely sober.

"I won't," he promised, and he stepped into the shock of cold.

φ

As he tilted down his narrow street, which still shimmered with coloured lights, he recollected Megan's well-intentioned remarks about the places he'd published, then something she'd said last week about all the bits and pieces of music floating in his head. He laughed out loud and looked up at the stars and decided they and the Christmas lights swimming in his vision were bits and pieces of those very songs spun into a bright swirl around him. When he stumbled too close to a parked car, its high beams flashed in warning and he laughed again, then steadied himself against a low wall while the world righted itself.

Well, it had been a good night, a rare night, and looking up and down the empty street at the winter trees and otherwise drab brick houses draped in starry brilliance he realized he couldn't say when he'd know such a night again. He thought of Carrie's bruised-sounding voice and the cool, refractive stare she'd levelled at Megan toward the end....

The cold went through him and he shuddered violently. But when he started walking again the warm room full of smiling women came to mind, and the phrases *all covered in sin* and *fucked with abandon* echoed around him.

φ

The holidays passed to one side of Omar as he worked away at the Mingus chapter. He'd amassed enough material for an entire book on Mingus, but the writing went ploddingly. Omar spent New Year's Eve at his desk while a light freezing rain ticked against his window. At midnight he turned off his desk lamp and closed his eyes. He listened and felt the darkness, like endless time, accrue around him. After several minutes he went out to the kitchen, poured some bourbon over ice, and found good jazz on the radio. The music, which he did not recognize, had a distant vitality, like a lost broadcast from a New York or L.A. ballroom that had been bumping around in the atmosphere's upper ions for decades. Now this freak storm had brought it out of the past at the exact moment when one year trailed into the next.

He listened to the ghostly music against the crystalline rain and lifted his glass in salute to the New Year, which might bring anything.

As January advanced, the winter turned bright and cold again. Then the temperature rose a few degrees and heavy snow once more filled the side streets and blanketed rooftops. Omar went out less frequently. With any luck, he'd finish the Mingus section by the month's end.

One clear, bone-jarringly cold Saturday he trudged out to buy a newspaper. The bustle and energy of College Street, even in the cold, surprised him. Furious white vapours rose from labouring automobiles; streetcars clanked and groaned between unbroken ridges of snow. The sunshine and blue sky had brought people out for brunch and shopping, and Omar walked slowly, half-dazzled by the snow glare and sparkling blue. Just ahead, at the light, a beige van pulled to the curb. A door slid open, a snugly-dressed figure hopped out and reached the sidewalk as Omar passed.

"Hey — "

He stopped and looked over his shoulder.

"It's Carrie. From Christmas."

She wore sunglasses and a red parka and a toque, but he knew the voice.

He said, "Carrie. Of course."

"How are you? How's your work going?"

He nodded automatically and shrugged. "Good," he said. "It's going good. Can't complain."

Their breaths rose between them as they stood on the sidewalk.

"We should get together sometime," she said.

"Sure. I'd like that."

She shifted a small nylon pack from her shoulder and pawed through it until she found a pen and a scrap of paper. She pulled off her glove, wrote on the paper, and handed it to him.

"Call me," she said, and she hurried across the street just as the light went green.

Omar looked at the note in his hand: *Carrie Coulter* – 555-9006.

He shoved it into his coat pocket and kept walking. At the Korean corner store he bought a newspaper and a carton of milk, then headed home.

For the rest of the day he worked hard and, he believed, well. One last push would put this section behind him. The knowledge that the book would be two-thirds finished would enable him to tackle the last third, the Coltrane section, with renewed vigour.

Later that night, while Omar was doing three days' worth of dishes, Harris phoned.

"So you're one of those guys who never returns his messages," Harris said.

"I guess..." Omar started, then made a musing sound. "You're right. Sorry, man. My head's in the work."

"Sure. Sure."

Omar laughed, content to let his friend believe he had secrets.

"That's all right," Harris went on in an easier tone, "I've been busy myself. We did a shoot in your part of town, took all of Thursday and Friday. And I've been working on these translations for my pal in France."

"What was the shoot?"

"Oh, just a bank commercial. It'll run on TV in the spring. And you're probably too out of it to have noticed my picture in the subway stations."

Omar admitted he couldn't recollect the last time he'd ridden the subway.

"You're a sick man, boss. You're headed to a very dark place. Although I have to say, you sound chipper tonight."

This surprised Omar.

"Well," he said, "I got something accomplished today." And then he thought of Carrie, the brightness of her face, the tight little smile beneath dark glasses.

"I just wanted to make sure you were still alive," Harris said. "I wanted to make certain you hadn't electrocuted yourself with the kettle or something."

After he hung up, Omar went to the closet and searched his coat pockets until he found the scrap with Carrie's number on it. He held it in his open hand like a coin or a promissory note: even without acting on it, *especially* without acting on it, the name and number represented a kind of currency against a debt of solitude and inwardness that might come due one day.

Strangely encouraged, he put the paper in the wide and shallow top drawer of his desk. From time to time during the following week, as he pounded on the typewriter, he thought of it lying in the space beneath the machine. But as he edged closer to the end of his chapter he forgot the paper and what was written on it.

Every morning he rose early and went straight to work. In mid-afternoon he pushed it away, pulled on a coat and hurried into the street, as if starved for air. For days he lived on coffee and eggs and cold cereal. One clear morning in late January he looked down from his window to the shrunken black figure of an old woman, Italian or Portuguese, creeping down his street with a rosary visible in her claw-like fist. A few yards behind followed a young family in Sunday clothes, the sallow-faced woman leading a small frilly girl by the hand while the wedge-shaped husband lagged even farther behind, car keys glinting in his enormous fist.

It's Sunday, Omar thought. He had totally missed Saturday. It had come and gone without the fact of *weekend* registering on him. Well, he was closing on the conclusion of his chapter. A couple of good days, and he'd be done. He watched the churchgoers and tried to guess which of the big Catholic churches in the neighbourhood they were headed toward – the solidly Portuguese one on Dundas or the more-or-less Italian church one street over and closer to College. He wondered if he envied the rhythm and stability of their lives. Certainly he had nothing against those qualities. Once, as recently as ten years ago, there had been similar, if not so deeply rooted, patterns in his own existence. Once, he'd been married. He'd had an office, or at least a cubicle, at the newspaper. Before that, he'd taught music history and journalism at a community college. He'd owned a car, had his own parking spot at the school. It all seemed at once amazing, given his current situation, yet wholly insignificant, considering the larger world's view that such tokens were obligatory for any competent adult. But one by one he'd given them up because they'd all run together in his head: office, parking spot, job. This blurring of relative values had turned him toward a single, pure activity – or at least the ideal of such an activity – that imposed its own system of priorities. A hierarchy, with music and its meaning at the top. Music and listening and turning one language into another, transcribing musical idiom into human speech, the latter always duller and a little below the mark but necessary, since it was always necessary to say why it was good to love and protect those elements in life one couldn't eat or drink or buy or sell or otherwise lay hands on. In one way, his work gave people permission to do nothing but listen. Without this permission, this endorsement, the hierarchy toppled; they lost a part of their humanity, and he – well, without this work he might find himself lost in a daze worse than the daze he laboured in, a daze of listening that nevertheless imposed a wholeness, a function.... And wasn't that all that most people had even at the best of times?

He drew a breath and let it out slowly. The street below was empty. He stood there with a transcription of a Mingus arrangement in his hand in the full late-morning light. The street below was like a snapshot of the inside of his head. A ghostly peace filled him. He shook himself and the words rushed back. Drawn to his desk again, he experienced an odd prescience of spring, but it lay beyond a gulf he could not think or will himself across.

φ

Omar finished the Mingus section the next Thursday afternoon. The messy handwritten pages must be revised and typed, but the hard part was over. He felt no particular relief or gratification: the all-important last third of his book lay ahead; an anxiety to begin it weighed on him every hour. But he couldn't bring himself to sit down and start. He napped dreamlessly through the winter afternoons and filled his nights with bad TV, staring for hours at the shopping channel or cooking shows. The white season outside his window was a blankness that had gotten into his head. He took books down from shelves, glanced at paragraphs, pressed the worn covers between his hands as if to absorb their warmth and revelation. One day Omar picked up a yellowed Everyman edition, flipped it open and randomly read these lines:

> That we are the breath and similitude of God, it is indisputable, and upon record of Holy Scripture; but to call ourselves a Microcosm, or Little World, I thought it only a pleasant trope of Rhetorick, till my near judgment and second thoughts told me there was a real truth therein.

He stared at the passage. Each word entered his mind like a stone dropping into a pond, disappearing instantly, leaving only a mysterious ripple. He re-shelved the book and turned the TV on to a vegetarian cooking program. An empty whiteness filled his window and he waited and wished for night to come.

Another week went by; he avoided his desk and entered his study only to answer the telephone. He made coffee and Jell-O and played sentimental records by Jack Jones and Acker Bilk and movie soundtracks from the Seventies.

φ

When he ran out of food he decided to buy a pizza slice on College Street before stopping at the supermarket. Perhaps he'd treat himself to a cappuccino at one of the nicer cafés after he'd eaten. As he stepped into the pizza place he realized what he really wanted was sleep; he thought he could easily sleep for the next forty-eight hours without missing anything or being missed. But where had this exhaustion come from? He'd done little but day-dream for the last two weeks. At the counter he ordered a slice of pepperoni and a Brio, paid for them, and waited at a table near the front window. On his way to the counter for the under-warmed slice, he bumped into a chair and stumbled. He took the pizza on its paper plate back to the window table and stared out while he ate. As he chewed the crust he realized his throat hurt. He swallowed carefully. Probably he was coming down with something....

Walking toward home, he felt the white sky bear down on him; the snowbanks looked old and scabrous, like ancient wounds on the earth. He shivered and hurried down his street. By the time he climbed the stairs to his apartment he was in the grip of a full-blown chill and his vision blurred at the edges. The door swung shut behind him; he dropped his coat and staggered shaking toward the bedroom. He sat on the bed, struggled to untie his boots and shed his clothing. He made himself look at the clock as he pulled at the covers. "It's four twenty-three in the afternoon," he said, as if knowing the time were a critical last act of con-sciousness. Then he closed his burning eyes and drew his knees to his chest and hugged himself in a shivering ball under the blankets. He reproached himself for making an inexcusable mistake. But almost immediately a thick and grainy darkness swallowed him and all his thoughts.

At first he seemed to be dead without having died, lying in a black emptiness outside of time where the world could not touch him and where he was satisfied not to be touched. Then, without waking him, the fever brought him up from the depths, rushed him up and up, then down, then up still higher on a giddy roller coaster that ran to the manic gallop of a Mingus tune or all Mingus tunes stitched into a perpetual loop that gathered momentum as it went, so that he rose and fell faster, then faster, on a seamless track. He hung on for dear life as the choruses plunged and rocketed up through the void; his breathing and heartbeat matched the music, became the music, and he knew he would die – his heart would burst, his brain would derail – if he did not get off this ride. Its loops dipped ever lower, swooping down so fast, tearing his breath away, then pitched him upward again, higher and higher toward a blinding light even more terrible than the darkness – and then he was awake, shaken and wet as if he'd been spewed from the maw of a musical Leviathan. He'd sweated through underwear and bedclothes and lay in a vile clamminess he hadn't the immediate strength to escape. Thank God he'd gotten off that ride: its lunatic strains faded into echoes as it chased itself into oblivion. He lifted a hand under the blankets and let it drop to his side. In a minute he'd rise and get some water. He raised his head, looked around. His eyes felt poached and the dim room existed at a distance like a burned-over swamp at twilight.

Rising ghostily, he shed his underclothes and bumped naked to the kitchen where he found a cup of water on the counter. The water tasted oily and brackish, like water from the swamp behind him. He put down the cup, and then, to his astonished alarm, he found himself in the hallway outside his apartment door, descending the stairs, naked but not cold, taking one step at a time under bare feet. Until he reached the door of the first-floor tenants, a noisy Portuguese family who often ran the vacuum cleaner at midnight and played their television too loud. But now from behind their closed door came the same fantastic amalgam of Mingus music, rolling nightmare choruses that grew louder and faster like a hellish dynamo that might explode the door and carry him off on another lung-bursting flight.

He stepped back and moaned, then instantly understood: *I'm still dreaming!* The door bulged with sound and he struggled upward, as if swimming through a slant of heavy yellow light straight up the staircase. The air was like sluggish water: he kicked and stroked slowly upward between floors, until at last he surfaced, gasping, in his damp bed.

This time he threw back the blankets and swung a leg out and pressed his foot to the cool floor, steadying himself like a drunk. In a moment he sat up and saw that he still wore his t-shirt and shorts. He glanced at the digital clock: 5:28 p.m. He had lost a day, or days. But he needed water and woozily stood, stripped off the clinging t-shirt and felt his way to the kitchen. He leaned over the sink and patted water over his face. From the dishes in the sink he extricated a glass and rinsed it and drank down two full glasses of tap water. In the cupboard above the sink he found a small plastic bottle of aspirin and swallowed two with more water. On his way back to the bedroom another chill struck; he pulled off his shorts and crept trembling to his bed. His teeth rattled like drum sticks on rims as he pulled the covers over his shoulders. When he closed his eyes again disjointed phrases and pictures flitted across his fevered brain. He heard guttural voices discussing the old Coconut Grove club in Los Angeles, he saw schools of tiny neon arrows swimming through the stained marble and porcelain men's room of a bus station... his gentle ex-wife, whom he never dreamed about, stood outside his window and gazed wordlessly up to where he should have been working on his book... "I'm sick," he told her from the distance of his bed, and then the aspirin kicked in, his trembling eased, and he passed into a flat and dreamless sleep.

φ

When he woke again the clock read 7:12 a.m. He was somewhat better, he thought, but his limbs ached and his eyelids felt like parchment. For a long while he lay staring at the ceiling, listening to the creaky-hinge whistle of starlings on his balcony. Then he sat up on the edge of his bed. On the floor his clothes were spread in a heap. Unsteadily he leaned and retrieved them, dropped them in a tall wicker basket near the door. What day was this? How long had he been out of it? Two days, he guessed, and by the weakness in him, the fuzziness of vision, he knew it wasn't over yet. He pulled on a clean t-shirt and some pyjama bottoms and socks. In the kitchen he drank more water, then rummaged through the refrigerator for a small container of yogurt. He sat and spooned it into his mouth; the wonderful coolness slid down his throat and soothed his stomach. He had turned no light on and the early morning house ticked in the silence. Going on Day Three, he thought, and his phone had not rung once. Or if it had, he'd slept through it. A panic struck. What if he died here? How long before they discovered his body? No one would open his door until – until a bad smell brought a tenant from above or below. What ignominy! By that point, practically speaking, it would all be the same to him, but the possibility held a secret horror – a vision of corruption – he did not want to contemplate.

He shook it off and searched his cupboards for something else to eat. Some digestive cookies and a packet of instant oatmeal came to hand. The cookies would do for a start; he put three on a plate and plugged in the kettle. A pot of green tea would set him up.

While the water boiled, Omar reflected on his febrile dreams, the sheer awfulness of them. Shadows of a milder but messily confused dream he'd had just before waking came back. It concerned Megan, he was certain. He tried to remember. Yes, definitely Megan, and to his waking dismay he realized there'd been sexual hijinks. In the dream he'd been potent, she'd been willing, but the rest faded into strange galleries and corridors.

The kettle shut off with a clack. He rubbed his eyes unhappily, then poured hot water over one green tea bag in a small brown pot. While the tea steeped, he stared at the pot and nibbled the dry edge of a digestive biscuit. He wanted no more dreams and hoped the worst was over. His skin felt tight and sore; his thoughts moiled in a brown fog a few feet to the right or left of him.

He poured a cup of the pale green tea and drank it greedily. The prospect of more fever, more dreams, frightened him. He ate the cookies and emptied the pot. When he rose from the table the faintest tremor went through him and he hurried back to the bedroom, on the brink of another chill.

Late in the afternoon he woke again, relieved he'd slept peacefully. A wan and granular light filled his apartment; it looked like an old sepia tintype of a stranger's rooms. For an otherworldly instant, he thought he heard that stranger's voice in the kitchen. He listened, then got up and went out to the kitchen table, panting lightly. He could feel the fever, just outside of him, waiting like a spirit to possess him when his guard was down.

On the fifth day he woke early again, made toast and tea, and went back to bed. Early in the afternoon he rose and drew a hot bath while he shaved. As he guided the disposable razor across his face he told himself that the illness had been worse than anything he'd known in years. It scared him with a new sense of the depth of his solitude, with dreams too awful ever to dream again. He still felt shaky and bronchial, but with any luck the fever had spent itself. Before climbing into the tub he turned on the radio balanced atop the plastic stool in the corner. With a tense shiver, he lowered his body into the hot water. It lapped at his chin as he slid lower and slowly relaxed, muscle by muscle. The water lifted four days of fever sweat from his flesh and he imagined it spreading away from him like a prismatic oil sheen. Slowly, as the radio played soft classical, his spirit began to uncoil and he spoke a few words to himself.

He glanced around at the dark pink tub and chrome fixtures, the cracked plaster ceiling and the dull grey tile floor. They seemed so foreign, nothing at all like a place where he could imagine himself living, and he recollected his horror of expiring here, of lying dead on the floor for days. Had his telephone rung once since he'd fallen ill? Once, maybe, a peripheral trill had sounded beyond the fever deeps, but no message had been left and he supposed whatever he'd heard had been hallucinated or dreamed. He closed his eyes in the rising vapours and lay corpse-like, his mind stuck between waking and sleep, until the music changed and something he'd forgotten tumbled into his mind on the boldly-stated opening piano chords. He knew the song, knew these chords like the back of his hand, but before he could say its name he beheld an element of wonder that flashed in front of him like his heart's true colours – an element of wonder or hope or the expectation of both that he realized he'd been living without for so long. Then he knew they were playing "My Favourite Things," the great Coltrane version he hadn't heard for years, perhaps not since his undergraduate days when he'd grown so tired of it he hadn't bothered to replace the record after someone filched it from his collection. But here it was again, the shape of the lost past come back on a present arc of wonder, not memory or nostalgia but wonder, like a brilliant companion of his youth returned to make him laugh, to make him brave, make him eager once more for all those moments that were their own immeasurable reward. Omar couldn't say why those initial piano phrases had struck him this way, but he caught his breath and followed the notes as if they were shiny pieces of hope that might lead him back, or forward, to something he hadn't, God forgive him, felt the absence of until just now. Just now, as he travelled back and forth on the transcending circuit of the music, he saw how far he'd come, how much he'd gained and how much he'd left behind. It was in the song. He'd heard it so many times, but he lay entranced as the piano went glowingly up and down the scales and Coltrane's soprano sax danced childlike around it, gave the melody wings, somehow reincarnated the score so that Omar heard it both again and for the very first time. He sat up in the water and attended: he heard the quartet reinventing the tune in a fury of creation, without losing its tunefulness or joy, and he had the sudden insight that they were creating new worlds out of sounds and associations, whole new worlds from the vast palette of human experience and the basic stuffs of wonder and song. Lying there, stretching his limbs, he saw himself as a boy in his father's house or running through a grade-school corridor, leaping high to touch the ceiling. This music existed then, and though he didn't hear it until much later he already knew the shimmer of the moment, the sunshine of wonder that was synonymous with the sound.

But now he heard direness in the music too, the subtle under-tone of Fate and fates, the collision and tangle of celestial forces that turned the wonder inside-out, that made every day dangerous and pivotal. Why had he never heard this before? Behind the new worlds Coltrane and his band juggled like toys, a sea of chaos boiled and churned like fever dreams....

The song ended and Omar subsided in the old pink tub, dazed, but more awake than he'd been for weeks. As he lifted himself from the water and reached for a towel, the news came on the radio. Sur-prised, he heard the announcer mention the date – late February already. So much time had vanished behind him, so much that would never come again. How much time had he given to his book? The sickness seemed to have burned up his old will and left a dry space of possibility. The space was finite, bordered on all sides by finite time, but it shone in his mind's eye, waiting to be filled with new music.

A wave of dizziness went through him. Omar propped himself against the tiled wall with one arm; with the other he clutched the damp towel to his chest. He wasn't entirely well yet, but he felt a small hopeful excitement. Any day now he'd begin the last chapter, the Coltrane chapter, and hadn't he just been given a bright omen about what lay ahead? Fifteen minutes ago he'd heard something he'd nearly forgotten and had ceased to expect, something that con-nected the world he would write about to the world he had forfeited so that he might write what he heard. For an instant he'd glimpsed the living bridge that the music, and then his words, could make between those two worlds: the get-ahead world of taxicabs and esca-lators sublimely bridged to the original source of all wonder. That's what he heard in the music. That's what he'd seen while his hands floated at his sides.

The dizziness passed. The bridge became a glittering mass of saxophone keys and typewriter parts, a musical promise and a metaphysical conundrum he'd have to solve at a future date. But he knew he was onto something. He couldn't say it or write it in sentences, not yet, but John Coltrane had spoken to him, and Omar believed that he would speak again.

Part II

Just before noon, Omar looked up from the typewriter and out at the March rain that spattered the bay window of his second floor study. The rain seemed to fall in counterpoint to the metal type that splashed the white paper. Rain, type, paper: they all, for an instant, had a significance, which had as much to do with what he'd written, the idea on the page, as it did with the mixed sounds of the rain and his typewriter. He'd been up half the night listening to Coltrane. In particular, he'd been playing several versions of "Nature Boy" over and over again. That song, like many of Coltrane's reinventions of standard tunes, provided a concise revelation of everything he had tried to do in his longer improvisations. The elements he wrestled with from, say, 1961 to the end were all present in these shorter forms. Spiritual ultimacy and temporal lyricism, melody and modality, they were all there. Omar had written that by flirting with chaos the musician had created a theory of apocalypse that bridged the historical and the personal, a theory of apocalypse that linked these several meanings into one. A music that purveyed the very feeling of being alive – the horrible pressure and ecstasy of the living moment – while likewise scoping out the collision and creation of worlds, the gorgeous wrack of Time. An epic accomplishment from a man who played the saxophone.

Feeling spacey, Omar stood and looked at the bare trees beyond the window, their grey skins shining with rain, their naked branch tips uplifted above the uniform row of houses across the street. Even today, overcast and drizzly, a springtime glow like yellow chalk glazed the clouds and heightened the earth colours in the old bricks of those houses. Just as he started to turn away his eyes fell on a single figure advancing down the sidewalk. A woman or girl in a mid-length black raincoat walked briskly, hands in pockets, a small nylon pack on her back. Her white face, slightly downcast, shone like a coin beneath rain-wet reddish curls. He saw all this in an instant, and something about her face or her determined, almost angry gait knocked Omar sideways in the head, so that his mind went blank and he heard a sort of clarion go up in the lucent grey-lemon air. He blinked and stared, glanced away from the window, then looked down again to the now vacant sidewalk. Only then he understood that he'd been looking at Carrie Coulter, whom he hadn't seen since that winter day when she handed him her number.

He resituated himself at the desk and stretched his hands on the keyboard and stared at a fragment of sentence in the middle of the page. Then he sat back and filled his lungs. For a second there, looking out at the world, at Carrie and all the known particulars of his street, everything had seemed to tilt. For a moment, sky and street had traded places, and Omar seemed to be sitting somewhere between them.

Omar rose and meandered to the kitchen, started coffee, leaned against the counter and tried to clear his head. All winter he'd been at it, writing and listening, listening and writing down what he thought the music meant. With the Coltrane chapter, the last chapter, it all seemed to be coming to a climax, and sometimes when he listened to those fantastic saxophone runs, those logic-bending "sheets of sound," the top of his head seemed to come off. It was almost too much for words, but words were the medium to which he'd committed himself. As he poured the black coffee from the carafe into his cup, he wondered if it had really been Carrie on the street. In the peculiar light, in the rain, he could have been mistaken. But the wet coppery hair and the nose, oddly flattened in profile like the carved likeness of some ancient conqueror, were surely hers. It surprised Omar that he had not thought of her for so long. At Christmas, when they met, she had seemed intelligent and well-spoken and was, by any literal standard, a lovely woman. And the evening spent with her family had been pleasantly boozy and diverting. So why hadn't he called her, even after she'd written down her number and invited him to stay in touch?

He held the steaming carafe, squat-bodied and snouty like an alchemist's retort, near his chest and squinted at it. He knew why he hadn't phoned her. In the course of that night at her house he'd recognized dissatisfaction and insecurity behind her glamour, qualities that could only make mincemeat of his own hard-won tranquility and singleness of purpose. Behind her opaquely blue eyes and inviting-but-haughty pout lay the kind of trouble that could desolate his entire enterprise. Moreover, her hunger and ambition were the very opposite of what he was about: her work was out in the world, in front of audiences, whereas he might go for days without leaving his house, struggling with a project for an audience so esoteric and hypothetical he dared not let himself think about it.

The carafe grew heavy in his hand and he set it on the range. He considered how it had come down through the decades, the artifact of a family extinct save for him and a vanished life. For an instant it shocked him to consider how thoroughly the past had slid away. Now, in his early forties, he was alone and slept well and lived from day to day on the momentum of his work. It was an absurd life for a capable adult. Yet he took pride in his solitude: it was like an athletic accomplishment he performed daily so that he might pursue that nearly incomprehensible thing he loved. Above all, he wanted no distraction from that pursuit.

Omar carried his cup into the study and planted himself at the desk. Fumbling through the shallow drawer that opened onto his lap, he eventually found the slip with Carrie's telephone number. He flattened it on the desk surface and stared at the girlish scrawl. What did he know about her? An actress in her late thirties who lived with her mother and her brother's young family and was perhaps frustrated by a lack of professional success. But maybe he was judging her unfairly from past experience with women who didn't know what they wanted, or wanted what didn't exist. His mind went back to the interminable winter and his spell of illness: the illness represented a kind of inversion of the season that had turned him inside out and flung him into spring. He still felt a little wobbly, and even frightened, from the sickness.

For a moment longer he stared at the slip of paper, then folded it in half, dropped it in his desk drawer, and went back to work on his manuscript.

φ

After dinner that night he settled himself in front of the old console television and before he knew what he was watching, whether it was a commercial or weekly drama or film, his attention went to the woman in the light-blue business suit who stood in an elevator with two executive-looking men. Co-workers under duress, they traded anxious scowls and stared up at the elevator signals as they rose from floor to floor. In the scowl Omar recognized Carrie, perfectly believable in the blue suit, her hair up, a portfolio clasped in her tense, white hands. The elevator stopped. The doors opened: in stepped the boss. Looks of pale horror all around. Despite the business clothes it was exactly the same Carrie he'd seen earlier that day, with her countenance similarly severe and strained. He felt bewildered, physically confused, as if he'd been spun around in his chair. But it was only a commercial for a new telephone service. It was only Carrie in a commercial. He slowly got out of the chair and turned on the light in his study and retrieved the piece of paper from the desk drawer. Without giving himself time to talk himself out of it, he phoned the number and waited while it rang two, three, four times. She wasn't in – naturally. Her voice message came on and it surprised him that it should belong to the woman on the sidewalk in front of his house and the face he'd seen on the TV screen five minutes ago. The fact that these were all the same person struck him as a marvel he should probably not ignore. He left a short matter-of-fact suggestion on her voice mail that they should meet for drinks in the near future. He said he hoped things were going well, mentioned his own number, and hung up. Immediately he felt relieved, as if he'd dispatched a responsibility that had nagged him for days. He wouldn't be surprised if she didn't return his call, but two sightings in one day had seemed to signify a challenge that he'd met: tomorrow morning he could go back to his work with a quiet mind, with a sense that his solitude and singleness of purpose were fated, ordained, and completely in the proper order of things.

Two days later, while he laboured at his desk in the afternoon, the phone twittered and he leaned and lifted the receiver without shifting his eyes from the sentence he'd just written.

"It's Carrie," she said. "I thought I'd never hear from you again."

He strained to refocus. The voice, hard but clear, did not seem like the voice of anyone he knew or was likely to meet. Then he remembered he'd called her.

"Omar?"

"Yes," he said. "I'm here. I was – in the middle of something."

"Shall I call back?"

"Oh – no! Not at all. I – that's fine. I'm glad you called."

"I kept thinking I'd bump into you again on the street."

For a second he envisioned such a meeting, and his heart quickened.

"My head's been wrapped up in my work all winter, trying to get this book on track. Time kind of got away from me." He waited, then, "How goes the acting business?"

She laughed a snirt of offhand laughter into the receiver.

"Pretty damn slow. I wanted to take a vacation, but I'm not going anywhere the subway can't take me." She spoke rapidly but clearly: "I think I just landed a beer commercial, though I'm probably jinxing it by talking about it. Oh," – and here her voice broke into a graceful wail – "I'm beyond jinxing. I've gone through so many cycles of luck it doesn't apply to me anymore."

Omar frowned and listened, trying to keep up as her voice rose and fell over the wire. Behind her bright, compulsive talk he detected a huskiness, an injured or outraged quality with a sexual base. He could easily imagine that voice making hysterical accusations or entreating through passion or tears. It was, he thought, an excellent acting tool.

She stopped suddenly. In a changed, almost suspicious, tone she asked what he'd been doing the moment she'd called.

Surprised, he said, "Nothing, really. I was just sitting here."

The silence that he heard between them, that he seemed to hold in his hand, struck him as pure and everlasting. He saw himself falling backwards endlessly into it. He coughed and said, "Thank God the weather has changed for the better. I thought winter would never end."

He thought he could hear her thinking before she said, "I love that feeling of possibility the good weather brings. Actually, I meant to call you earlier. It's March break for the kids and I'm taking my niece to the museum tomorrow. I thought you might want to come along. We could get a drink or something after we take Ivy home." She hesitated. "It's odd to think of you living just down the street."

He hadn't thought about it before, but she was right. Since he'd moved here last summer the street had become fundamental to his outlook, his ability to function. He hadn't yet defined it to himself, but the street was a constant that comforted him, and now he knew she was on it.

Then something else occurred to him, a gear shifted, and he hurried to tell her that he needed the afternoons for his work: he'd love to accompany them to the museum, but he was up against a deadline of sorts and perhaps he could meet her later in the evening for a drink? Without a trace of disappointment Carrie said that sounded fine and why didn't he stop by her house around seven the next evening.

He hung up and blinked at the pages scattered around his type-writer, some of them jammed with longhand scribble. Often, when he hit a rough patch, he'd put the typewriter away and compose with a pen – only that type of pen, and always during the same hours each day. How eccentric had he become? He had just turned down a charming afternoon on a spring day with a highly attractive woman so that he could keep to his writing schedule. Or was he afraid of something? For so long his world had consisted of music and writing, listening and rendering the meaning of music into accessible prose. But since starting the Coltrane section he'd felt one step away from saying what he really meant, what he ever-so-tentatively knew. The music suggested an idea, and the harder he tried to realize the idea as language, the more distant and furtive the idea became. The ideas came readily enough when he really listened; doors opened every time he turned his ear to what Coltrane was saying. But in the writing he was always dancing on the precarious edge of abstraction, always a step or two behind in the translation. Often he felt like he was chasing his own tail, but he knew he was on to something, and what he chased was more like the tail of a comet. Well, with a little luck it would come to him. In music or in writing, a little luck made all the difference, and he still believed that by paring away the superfluous concerns and ambitions of life he had made room not only for the music but also for some luck to shine through.

φ

Omar left his house Thursday evening as a damp chill rose from the street. After hours at his desk, the raw air felt good against his face, and he congratulated himself on retaining a sense of delight in the actual world of trees and sidewalks and old, upright houses with almost no space between them. A cold fragment of moon scraped the bare trees above the street lamps. Carrie was right, it was odd that they lived on the same street, on the same side, maybe two hundred yards between them. Odd to think of her living in the basement of her mother's house with her brother's family filling the second and third floors. A richly peculiar household it seemed to Omar, a place of niceties and yearnings, empty bottles and fresh flowers. That Christmas night, when Megan brought him there, he'd been struck by the fact that a world of seasonal observances and family rituals still existed, and by how far he'd drifted from its ordinary reassuring rhythms.

Now he walked down their street and decided his good mood was fuelled by something like anticipation, for this night and the new season in general. The inevitable summer that was coming. He reached Carrie's house and stood before it. Lights blazed on the ground level and from the single basement window. Again he wondered why he'd waited so long to arrange this meeting. It wasn't that the household he'd seen in the winter had failed to intrigue him. If anything, there was too much going on: too much talent and intelligence and intensity compressed under one roof. And something in Carrie's face had worried him. A face that scowled more often than it smiled, and the eyes almost too blue, too bright and opaque.

Nevertheless, that Christmas night, in the cloud of feminine wit and wine, he had enjoyed himself thoroughly and been one of the last to leave. And with spring on the horizon, after being immersed in words for so long, he had to admit it was refreshing just to stand before Carrie's house in the row of houses that lined his street. You couldn't miss her place because of the children's names, Tyler and Ivy, inscribed in the concrete base of the steps. A precise, small voice in his head said that if he walked straight home and telephoned a polite excuse it would save him time and money and precious energy he needed for his book. Both instinct and experience told him this was true.

But surely he'd been too much alone. This was equally true.

He went up the narrow walkway to the porch and pushed the buzzer near the brass mailbox.

A shadow appeared behind the small window in the second door, and Carrie opened both doors, her face bright and blank around the smallest smile.

"You're here exactly on time," she said, stepping back, motioning him in.

"I guess that's bad."

"What? Oh, no. Not bad, but I'm not quite ready yet. You might as well come downstairs while I finish changing."

He followed her through her mother's kitchen, small and cozily cluttered with teapots, ashtrays, half-empty packages of Peak Freens, then down the stairway at the back of the house. Carrie's long main room was comfortably furnished with large soft chairs and bookcases. Something about its underground dimness and muted lamplight reminded Omar of an out-of-the-way smoking or reading room in an art museum. She gave him a chair at a work table covered with computer, fax machine, pens and papers and poured him a short glass of Irish whiskey that her brother had brought her from a business trip. For a few minutes she chatted absently about an audition she'd had that day, then she left him with his drink while she changed her clothes in a smaller adjoining room. He glanced about at the homey knick-knacks and artsy details, the drawing pencils and sketch pads and, most astonishingly, the plaster cast of a full set of human teeth that crowned a stack of record albums in the corner. He took in the magazines and photographs and a large snow dome that contained an elegant, tragic-looking angel. On the shelf behind the computer stood a framed black-and-white studio photograph of her mother as a young woman, the hard edge of her glamour and vitality shining through the dimness of the room. He stepped across the room and lifted the plaster teeth, weighty and complex, like an artifact of the occult. He looked down and saw they'd been sitting on the worn black cover of the Coltrane – Johnny Hartman album from 1963.

Carrie emerged and stared at the cast in his hand.

"Those are mine," she said. "I mean, they're my teeth. I had to get them capped when I got into acting seriously."

Back in the winter, on the street, he had noticed her perfect and perfectly white teeth.

"I grind them at night," she said. "After investing all that money, I have to wear a tooth guard when I sleep. Are you a grinder?"

"Probably," he said. "Is that your Coltrane record?"

She shifted her stare to the stack of albums. "Those? Those belonged to my father." She reached and took a small gulp of whiskey from his glass. "Mom still has a turntable that works, we use it quite a bit."

"It's a classic recording."

"I guess so," she said, but she was staring morosely at her plaster teeth again. He handed them back to her. "Just one of those costly investments I've made in this so-called career," she said flatly.

She set the teeth back on the record stack.

"Whatever happens with your career," Omar said, "you'll always have great teeth."

She frowned and flashed him a dangerous look. "Yeah," she said. "That's right."

She put on her coat, he finished his drink, and they went out. The evening was colder now; muzzy low clouds had settled over the rooftops and trees and they glowed bluish in the city night. At the end of the street, trolleys hurtled and pedestrians crossed. Omar thought of summer amusement parks and his very first date with a girl, when he was fifteen or sixteen, at such a park full of rickety old rides and vast dimly lit arcades with mechanical games and ancient pinball machines. It had happened several lifetimes ago and he recollected it as an event from antiquity.

Carrie said something about how the sky had looked earlier in the day. She tried to describe how the clouds had hung in layers. They both looked up as she spoke, and Omar breathed deep.

He let her choose the restaurant on the next block – an Italian place that looked long and cavernous through the front glass. As they stepped inside, a well-dressed man at the bar gave them a smiling thumbs up. A uniformed waiter ushered them through the pleasant shadows toward the back. Only two or three other couples sat scattered about in the darkness, a candle flickering on each table.

Carrie selected and approved the wine. She swished it around in her glass and tasted it. The waiter leaned over the table, uttered a short, suave query in Italian. Carrie said, "*Si*," and the waiter poured red wine into their glasses.

After they ordered their food, Carrie asked, "Who was your friend at the bar?"

"My what?"

"At the bar. I thought you knew him," she said, lifting her glass in one hand.

"Oh, that guy – " Omar looked around. "I never saw him before. Sometimes people think they know me. Now that you mention it, it was kind of odd."

They talked easily enough through their meal, about their work and the frustrations they faced in this city. Both of them had lived in New York ten years ago, and they traded stories about their experience and how emotionally impoverished this place seemed after Manhattan.

"Everybody here expects too much," Omar told her. "The women are aloof and beautiful and the men are fussy and parsimonious. Everyone's panicked that they're missing the essence in this life." He shrugged. "On the other hand, they're probably right. Whatever's important is probably not happening here."

Carrie listened with a faint scowl and half-lidded eyes. Omar turned the topic to her business. She began slowly, then geared into a full-scale harangue about actors and casting directors and agents, how she spent her days rushing from audition to audition, hopes rising with callbacks, hopes dashed when they chose someone else. He nodded and poured the last of the wine into their glasses.

"What about you?" she said, pausing to sip. "What makes you want to write about music?"

He swallowed some wine and looked at her.

"Something happened to me back in the winter that might signify," he said, and he tried to explain his post-illness bathtub epiphany. He tried to tell her how the music had seemed fresh and wondrous, but rich with memories too.

"I'm sure it had something to do with being so sick and alone," he said, "but it was like the music went right through me. Like it filled my body. It brought back all kinds of stuff and made it new at the same time and I knew that I was getting better. I knew I was going to be all right."

He caught Carrie's small, tight smile and added, "I guess any song can have that effect, if it's the right song. That just happened to be the right song for me." He laughed, self-consciously. "That's probably more answer to your question than you wanted."

Her smile broadened. "I can't remember the question."

He laughed again and assured her he was not accustomed to talking so much.

"It's what comes from living alone."

He glanced up, suddenly afraid he'd revealed too much.

Carrie made a sound of annoyance. She said, "The only time I have to myself is when I'm riding public transit. Too many people in my house."

Omar looked at her dramatically shaped face in the candlelight and wondered at the broken, angry sound she'd made in her throat.

As they left the restaurant Omar realized he'd been served the wrong dish. He'd ordered pasta with clams, but they'd brought him calamari.

They strolled by dimly lit restaurants and bars. Carrie said, "Last summer I did this movie where I played a nymphomaniac. It was the first graphic sex I've ever done in front of the camera." She said this like an aside or afterthought as they walked and glanced at the wavering faces inside the restaurants. "I guess it was an okay thing to do," she said, "because I was on top. The woman was the victimizer for a change."

Omar supposed there might be strictly technical reasons for putting the woman on top in such a movie, but he didn't say anything. She seemed to be asking him to ask her more about all of this, but he only nodded as they walked.

"They might screen it at the festival in the fall," she said.

The fall. Would he be around in the fall? Would his book be done?

Back at Carrie's house, they lingered at the foot of the steps where the children's names were written in the cement. She leaned close quickly and kissed his face. Then she said goodnight and ran up the walkway to the porch.

Omar drifted slowly toward home and tried to remember the kiss. He tried to remember the scent of her skin, a perfume he hadn't noticed until her lips touched his face. He walked down the quiet street trying to bring it back. It had come and gone so fast.

The next morning he reimmersed himself in stacks of manuscript pages. Later in the day, when he stood to stretch, he recollected his evening with Carrie with something like surprise, the encounter seemed so distant and unlikely. As he made dinner, he recalled the man who had given him the high sign at the bar. Now it clicked: the signal was simply one male congratulating another for arriving with a glamorous woman. God, he'd been out of action for so long he had missed the obvious, the simple dumb stuff that made the world go round. Anyone who kept regular company with Carrie would get that on a steady basis. A man's nerve would have to be rock solid. Omar decided he had no interest in testing himself.

But throughout the next week, almost every time he turned on the television, he caught her commercial, or just the end of it as he cruised the dial: her face from the side, then dead on, Carrie working the camera, working hard for a few seconds of potent expression. One night her face came through the static of his day on a new slant and he thought he saw a face of genuine suffering, the face of her actual unhappiness, which was striking and sexual and even elegant in its pain, and it hurt him to behold this shining through the banality of the advertisement. It seemed incredible, somehow wonderful, that this face had pressed his with a kiss, and it hurt him again to behold its secret pain.

Omar hadn't known many actors before, and he supposed the good ones could turn themselves inside out to sell a hamburger. But the commercial disturbed him, and he began to avoid the channel that ran it most often.

φ

On a bitterly cold night, a few weeks after their dinner date, as Omar walked along College Street, he heard a peal of laughter from across the street and he knew it was Carrie. He peered at the dark figures in front of a pizzeria and picked her out, with a man. The night was crystalline; the cold went through him as though he were made of paper. Omar put his head down and hurried on, grateful he didn't know her better, believing as he walked that further knowledge would be nothing but pain and distraction in the wake of that full-throated, nearly ferocious note that had carried on the frigid air. And as he walked he felt relieved that it was not his pain, that it would come to someone else, perhaps to the man at her side.

That night he dreamed about Carrie. He dreamed she was on the old *Ed Sullivan Show* singing "Dream a Little Dream of Me," in a voice that was slow and sweet and a little clotted, charmingly, like a winsome teenager. In the dream she stood in a pastel light on a pop-art stage and she wore a sleeveless tangerine dress; her voice penetrated his sleep, his huge accrued solitude, like a ray of sunshine in a shuttered room or a luminous fish sliding elegantly through an inky sea. Her role in the dream was so unlike the persona of the TV commercial that it stayed in his mind into the next day.

That afternoon, prompted by the dream or what he'd seen the previous evening, he went to his telephone and left a message suggesting that they catch a movie some day soon. He told himself that enough time had passed since their date that calling her was no big deal. Again, after he'd made the call, what he felt was closer to relief than to anticipation, so that when she phoned back two days later to suggest a film it took him a moment to recollect that it had been his idea. Still, the sound of her voice, the voice that had sung in the dream, brightened his day, like an unexpected bit of good weather.

Carrie suggested they meet Saturday night at her house and take the streetcar to an old rep theater a short ride from their neighbourhood. The days were getting longer and the sun had just begun to set when he left his apartment and started toward Carrie's house. She opened the door with that half-angry bafflement on her face.

"You're nothing if not punctual," she said. "I phoned your place five minutes ago to say I'd come down there first."

"Oh, well," he faltered, "that would have been fine."

"Never mind," she said, and she vanished into a back room.

Her mother stepped into the hall and asked him if he cared for a quick drink. He said he'd better not. Then Carrie's tiny nephew, Tyler, came down the stairs and gazed up at him. Omar had the uneasy sense of having made a wrong move by arriving at precisely the appointed hour.

She reappeared in her overcoat, a knapsack over her shoulder. They said goodnight to her mother like any fresh teenage couple and went out to catch their streetcar. Carrie walked briskly, always a little ahead of him, and talked in a casual monotone that was not particularly personal or impersonal.

Omar smiled and cursed himself for arriving on time. That had been a gaffe. She had wanted to come to his place first, and who knew how the agenda might have altered in that case?

After they'd walked a few blocks, he forgot his discomfiture and followed her voice, a pace or two ahead, and began to enjoy the evening. They missed one streetcar that rocked by, on down the track into the mellowing dusk.

Carrie veered into a convenience store to buy a soda for the movie and to look for an Easter egg colouring kit for her niece and nephew. Omar saw that the kids were a big part of her life. He could imagine them as adults, trading stories about their eccentric aunt, the actress. No egg colours at this store, but she loaded her pack with soda and strode out into the night. Omar trailed after, intrigued and astonished by the street: the light had gone to pink and peach, and all the shabby storefronts stood out in distinct relief. Omar opened his leather jacket as he rambled after Carrie.

"Easter's in a week and it feels like summer," he said.

"Here comes our car," Carrie said, and she ran for the stop.

They climbed into the long empty trolley, lit in warm orange and brown, and ambled back to the very last, long seat. Carrie, alert and nervous, pointed out a derelict hotel, painted an unlikely aquamarine, where she'd once gone drinking with a man who'd directed her in a film in which she'd had a feature role. Omar thought he should ask her more about the film, or the man, but the passing street, washed in ocean blues and flamingo pinks, reminded him at once of a night in Los Angeles years ago and a night he'd yet to spend in another seaside town somewhere ahead of him, perhaps this very summer.

"What a sunset!" he said. "When I'm old and senile in some home this night and this street will come back to me, and I'll say, 'Who was that woman with me then?'"

Carrie sniffed and jutted her chin.

"Right," she said, "and that will be after we've been married twenty years."

Omar looked at her and felt a vague prescience, a premonition of a premonition that might have everything or nothing to do with this woman.

They got off at the next stop and turned down a side street that led them into a neighbourhood of shops and Catholic churches with Polish and Ukrainian signs in the windows. Carrie stepped inside an odd little bakery where she found the egg colouring kit. Since they still had time to kill before the movie, she suggested they find a bar. The magic light had bled from the sky; the night was already heavy and black. They peered into various drinking establishments before settling on a narrow Polish bar done wholly in varnished browns and dull reds. The place looked ancient and dim; eight or nine seedy-looking middle-aged men were drinking sullenly at the counter. The faces were unshaven, slightly stunned, but all eyes under swollen lids followed Carrie to the back of the room.

"Is this okay? Will this bother you?" Omar asked her.

"I've handled worse."

One slightly haggard but smiling young woman stood behind the bar. Her good nature seemed to keep the men docile. Carrie ordered two pint-bottles of Polish lager and put the cash on the counter. Omar said he'd get it, but she insisted. Suddenly happy with the place, they looked around at the wooden liquor cabinets with intricately paned fronts behind the bar. Omar said it reminded him of old neighbourhood bars in New York. Unfamiliar Polish music drained out of the spookily lit jukebox behind them.

"This is good," Omar said, taking it in. "This is nice."

"Yes, it's a good place," she agreed. "It has a feeling of possibility. It makes you feel something is coming."

"It feels," he said, "like we're in a different time, or a different city. Something about the light earlier, and this bar, something — "

"Uncanny," they said at precisely the same instant.

Carrie did a double take and Omar laughed. The coincidence actually seemed to make Carrie uneasy.

"You wear a pinky ring," she said, deliberately changing the subject.

He glanced at the ring on his little finger and said, "Don't worry, I'm not an engineer."

He might have told her how his mother, on her deathbed, had taken the ring off her hand and put it on his. Instead, he plunged into a story about a bar he knew in Manhattan. Then he asked her again about her time there almost a decade ago. She talked haltingly, as if that time had been definitive, and troubled. She told him how close she'd come to making it, to getting a TV series, how the city was much more threatening then. She asked him why he hadn't stayed in New York or California when he spoke as if he'd enjoyed both places.

Omar met her eye and said, "I get bored easily."

She turned her head and he realized he'd blundered, he'd said something strictly for effect that had frightened her. He might have truthfully reported that he left places because he'd made them impossible to live in. In the past, he'd followed a sort of emotional scorched earth policy that required him to cut his losses and move on. That was the past, he might have added, and things were different now. But he explained none of this, and instead asked the young woman for two more pints. He paid for this round and drank off half the glass quickly.

The music from the jukebox changed: Omar recognized a tune he hadn't heard since high school – it was a song of melancholy, wistful yearning and inevitable disappointment. It told of a man waiting in the dark for a woman who would never show. Sitting there, hearing it again, Omar experienced a poignant ache, a perplexing nostalgia, not for any person or time, but for that rarefied pain he had so effectively removed from his life. In his youth, that pain had been part of the pleasure of being in love. Back then, everything registered on the raw nerve of his spirit; the pain was dense, sublime, it connected him to the living world. Back then it left no scars. He hadn't felt that nerve in years, he guessed. Not really. This was a mixed blessing.

He watched Carrie finish her drink. The earlier moment of rapport had vanished. He sat there trying to feel it. The music swirled around them, a melancholy oboe in the night, the singer waiting in the dark, knowing the woman will never come. It wasn't, Omar thought, the culpability of an individual or a gender, but merely the futility of trying, always trying, bending the will toward the impossible longing of the heart. Again, he felt surprised he'd forgotten that feeling so completely, and equally surprised that something of it had come back with the music, and Carrie, and the night.

"It's beginning to get to me," she said.

"What? What is?"

"All this staring, like they hadn't seen a woman in months."

Omar looked at the row of rumpled men gazing dully and un-abashedly through the blue haze of cigarette smoke. For some reason he recollected what she'd told him about the movie she'd made last summer.

"Okay," he said. "Let's get out."

He left a tip for the long-suffering woman behind the bar and they maneuvered down the narrow room to the door. He felt the deadened eyes follow them to the street.

"Well, you made their night."

Carrie grimaced. "I've been chased and hounded my whole life," she said.

Omar glanced at her and felt the chilly bite of the darkness. He could easily imagine her turning that tone on him, telling him to stay away, to stop calling. He could imagine a scene on their street, a chance meeting, where she wheeled and demanded to know if he'd spotted her from his window and had rushed down to inter-cept her; he could hear the crazy righteousness in her voice, the idiot confusion in his reply. Back in the bar, for a moment, they'd shared the wavelength, they'd had a moment together. Now they were outside of it, walking in the renewed cold, walking quickly; Omar, once more, half a stride behind.

The theater was a carefully restored building with a little glassed-in ticket booth that extended to the sidewalk. Omar admired the old seats and the fixtures, but the movie itself was overly serious and manipulative and somehow compounded the failure of the evening. When they stood on the street Omar felt thwarted: whatever they'd hoped for when they'd spoken of possibility had been deflected.

They stood in the cold and waited for the streetcar. Carrie shivered and for no apparent reason started talking about her father.

"He drank himself to death," she declared. "Literally. Half his stomach was removed and he kept on drinking. It was like suicide."

Omar nodded mechanically as she spoke. There were two things, he thought, you didn't want to hear a woman say about her father. She had just told him one of them.

They saw the streetcar coming down the long, broken darkness of the street. It groaned to a halt; the doors opened and they climbed up and dropped their fares into the box. Carrie sat beside a window and suddenly changed the topic to a casual acquaintance who had pressed her for a coffee date; when she had finally agreed and gone to the appointed meeting place the man had walked by with another woman, giving Carrie no sign of recognition.

Omar looked at her. She was telling him these awful stories, the night had gone flat, but the weird thing was that he still enjoyed her company. He still felt that something was coming. Something he hadn't guessed yet.

"And that threw you?" he asked her. "Being cut by someone you barely knew, someone you weren't hot to see in the first place? You must get more than your share of attention in that way."

"What do you mean?"

"I just can't believe that you'd feel insecure in that department."

She trained her blue eyes on him, then looked out the window again.

"Depends on the day," she said.

Omar followed her gaze to the night-time city sliding by the window. She knew the place so much better than he; she'd grown up here, had had friends and lovers who lived on this street or the next and understood the unspoken social rhythms in ways he never could.

"You know," she said, "I knew your voice long before we met. There was a night last summer when you and Megan were walking home after the bars closed. I was in bed in the basement, must have been two in the morning. I had an audition the next day, and I heard Megan and this other voice that reminded me of New York. It was you. You don't know the power of your own voice. It carries through everything."

He had forgotten this episode entirely. Back in August, on a very hot night just after he'd moved to the neighbourhood, he had been bar-hopping with Megan. Now he remembered wandering slowly home in the small hours, drunk and delighted with his new street. He remembered swaying against Megan as he stared up at the night-blue city sky, which pulsed with satellites and tiny blinking airplanes that crawled between the trees.

"You stood out there laughing and talking until I got out of bed and went up to the deck on the third floor for a cigarette. I could hear your voice moving slowly down the street."

Carrie gave a sniff, not exactly laughter.

"Paulette heard me and came out with a bottle of wine. It was so hot we sat up the rest of the night drinking and smoking."

As they rode in the streetcar, Omar imagined Carrie on that other night, lying in the dark below him, listening, then putting on an old shirt and going upstairs for a smoke. He could see her leaning on a railing, peering through the dark toward his house. He could hear Paulette's quiet voice and the sound of wine filling a glass. Would he ever see that deck? Would he ever join them there on a summer's night?

"I'd totally forgotten all that," he said.

Carrie smiled grimly and stared out the window.

When they disembarked near their street, she said, "I guess I'm too tired to get another drink. Suddenly I don't feel well."

"That's fine," he said as they walked. He felt a slight sinking, but he'd expected this. "That's all right. It turned cold again, didn't it?"

They walked to her house and stopped where the sidewalk met the steps.

"Goodnight," she said, and she stepped up and away from him. She stared down at him, her brow constricted. In a voice both sad and petulant, she said, simply, "Thanks for coming out."

Then she was gone and he stood there blinking down at the names of her niece and nephew spelled in the cement.

φ

Just before dawn, Omar sat up in his bed, wide awake. He recognized the agitation of spirit that had roused him, remembered it from other days like the song he'd heard on the jukebox the previous night. And like the song, it was an agitation that even now, stumbling out of bed and begrudging lost sleep, he felt nostalgic for, as though he'd despaired of ever feeling it again.

He went to his desk and tried to work. His mind blanked and revived, blanked and revived. His pen went dry, and as he held the useless instrument in his hand he had the sudden intuition that Carrie was also awake, prowling silently through her mother's house. He saw her pulling on an overcoat and stealing into the backyard to smoke a cigarette in the mist.

"Shit," he said, and he rapped his head lightly with a knuckle.

He flung the dead pen in a waste basket and put a Coltrane record on the turntable in the other room. Still a vinyl guy, he said to himself, not proudly but with the resignation of someone who'd tried the newer technologies. He listened to "Naima" and read the back of A Love Supreme, the faded album cover like a parchment scripture in his hand. This text, he'd written in his new book, constituted a raw, genuine document in American cultural and religious history. As priceless and pivotal as, say, Leaves of Grass or Walden. A kind of American psalm that might, with the music, form the basis of a new faith in the new century. With the music, Coltrane's words created a complete interior experience, a kind of New Testament, if only we had ears to hear it.

Still, the worn cardboard made him feel old. And why not? He had been tried with time, had pushed and failed and pushed until he'd learned the limitations of human will, where it might be effectively applied and where it only screwed things up. In matters of human intimacy, for instance. But one could make books or music out of will and keep some kind of love and wonder alive in one's private soul. Real art required both will and love, and both must be protected somehow.

He listened to the sweet, seemingly aimless melody as the morning brightened. He pondered Carrie's sudden disenchantment of the night before. What was that about? She seemed to be testing him, or the situation. She seemed to be walking through it, to see how it felt, or waiting for him to produce a set of actions she could play off of. He had the idea, suddenly, that maybe that's what actors did instead of think: they walked through a situation to see how it felt, and if it didn't feel right they just kept walking. He had confused or bored her last night, and she'd ended the scene. Something like that.

What the hell.

He stretched out on the couch and listened to the music. It occurred to him objectively, and perhaps for the first time, that without the music he would surely perish. It made a pure balm, a comfort that registered physically, in his nerves and skin. It was what he had instead of love. Or, it was a kind of love that kept him centered, that held him to the planet. Only the caress and revelation of sound kept him sane and connected to this earth. Whether or not it would suffice in the long run was an open question.

At noon, he phoned Harris.

He described the outing with Carrie; how, despite the warning signs, he felt frustrated at not being able to stay on the wavelength with her. She seemed to like him, but the connection kept getting jammed.

"Let me tell you, boss," Harris began. "You absolutely do not want to get involved with an actor."

It was hard for Omar not to picture his friend's large, handsome head as he listened to his voice – the voice of a TV anchor or FM announcer. If Harris could forget his poetry habit and put serious energy into his modelling work he might generate a real career.

"Don't love an actor unless you can love her world, which I wager you know little about," Harris said. "I'm telling you, it's all hype and silliness, until you meet one tortured beauty selling her soul piecemeal to the industry. And then, after you sink into her world and suffer a thousand hurts on her behalf, it's still hype and foolishness. When it's over you'll hate her and yourself for wasting good emotion on the whole circus. I'm telling you. I know."

Omar exhaled and closed his eyes. "I guess," he said.

"I know, boss. Listen to me. Don't go down that road."

"But what else is there?" Omar asked him. "Sometimes I feel like I live in a vacuum."

"Hey, whatever it is, I know that most of the time you're happy to live there. You have your peace of mind; you get your work done. You're way ahead in the game, believe me."

Omar listened to the humming silence between them.

"Maybe it's an age thing," he said. "Some days I feel like time is running out for me. I feel like it's now or never."

"Oh, give me a break," Harris laughed. Then, more soberly: "Hell, some days I feel that way myself. That's just normal."

Harris was thirty-eight. Carrie's age. It seemed to Omar to be an age of portent and heavy meaning, the exact age when the bonuses of youth – imagination, vitality – are traded for the more solid foundations of an adult life. The former, in most cases, were waning anyway, and to exchange them for a good job or a better house made sense, although Omar could barely remember what was going on in his own life at that age.

"At any rate," Omar continued, "when you're younger, you get into the game to get something particular out of it, something like love or happiness that's outside of the game. Later, it's strictly the game for the game's sake."

He could hear Harris put something crunchy into his mouth.

"And what's the game?" Harris asked. "What's the game for you?"

"I don't know. I guess it's getting something out of the music and putting it into books. I guess it's something like that."

"Right. And what else is there? Love? Marriage? Swimming pools? Barbecues? What else is there other than your game?"

"Well, I'd take any of the above. No, there has to be something else. Funny, you start with love and the banalities automatically follow. But no, there has to be more."

"Like what?"

"I don't know," he said. "A sense of shared wonder? I'm not sure."

Harris paused, then chewed on the crunchy stuff again.

"I don't know, chief. Is she offering anything like that? Is she capable of it?"

Omar laughed. What he liked about Harris was that he might show up beside a mountain stream in the Tilley Hat catalogue, a look of visionary enlightenment on his chiselled face, but in his own life he weighed his investments and expenditures very practically.

"In any event," Harris said, "the smart thing for you is to avoid complicating your life, at least until your book is finished. Why rock the boat? You're in a good work groove. Don't jinx it."

As he hung up, Omar recalled Carrie saying that she was beyond being jinxed. Did she really think she was bad luck? For herself, or the people around her? Undoubtedly, he'd be out on a limb with such a woman, a woman who flashed all the warning signs whenever he saw her. Every outing was a gamble. It was, he told himself sternly, *fucking with abandon* and there would surely be a price to pay.

φ

It wasn't difficult for Omar to forget Carrie and burrow back into his work and solitude. He was devoted to his solitude, and he believed that his work required it. He had learned to cloak himself in a music of deep solitariness, a deep blue music with its own rhythm and meaning that welled in his tranquil heart. Sometimes, in his sleep, he went so far down into the music – which was also a kind of silence – that he experienced a rapture of the deep that took him away on dark currents, that carried him to a moment of crisis and decision where the inevitability and appeal of dark infinity beyond consciousness beckoned to him and he knew he must choose: either wake himself or flow through the dark on that current that ran to infinity at the bottom of his soul. And each time he woke with a sluggish start, like a man who swims up from a sinking ship and finds himself on a beach with the familiar blood-rhythm of surf in his brain.

He wondered at these profoundly deep sleeps, but he always came out of them feeling calm and renewed, a little sad, but ready to work on the book that he hoped might contain at least a trace of this mysterious, final music.

For days he worked feverishly. When his phone went off late one afternoon he looked at it as though he'd forgotten its existence and tried to recollect when he'd spoken into it last. He lifted the receiver: Megan's breathless, overloud greeting rang in his head. He spoke a few words, then she plunged in: "So I met someone new," she said, almost smugly. "What a doll. Omar, listen to me, this guy is it. A perfect match. I can hardly believe it."

"What about the other one? Whatshisname? The one you were telling me about?"

"Who? Oh, yeah, Lance. Well, I feel a little bad about him. It kind of ended in a hurry. But it was inevitable. There was no future there, you know? But this one – his name's Gary – is definitely a step up." She laughed woozily. "For one thing, he's taller than me. And he has his own car!"

After she'd talked herself into exhaustion, she abruptly signed off and hung up.

Omar looked at the receiver in his hand.

In the kitchen, he poured a glass of juice, then stepped through his bedroom and out onto the bare balcony. The spring morning was bright and cold. Nascent green quivered in the grass below. Birds chirped in season. Soon, he felt better. He reminded himself, again, of the peculiar similarities between Megan and Carrie and rededicated himself to his book, to the rapturous music at the heart of it.

On a Friday afternoon, rooted to his desk, his pen jittering across the page, a distant sound, an almost otherworldly vibration, came through his window on the smoke-coloured light and his pen hand braked, his head came up and turned toward the light. He had been writing about the nearly incomprehensible leap from church music to bop, how so many of the innovators and giants had been schooled in the ecstatic poetry of the Protestant hymn with its Old Testament myths and New Testament eschatology. He'd been embedded in these thoughts when he heard real music, faintly, welling in the distance. He looked down through the window and saw well-dressed pedestrians filing toward College Street, as if to a wedding or a funeral. Omar hated to break his writing rhythm, but this called for a look. Just a look. He donned his jacket and jogged down the stairs to the street and followed a family in their Sunday best toward the larger thoroughfare.

At College he beheld an uneven wall of humanity stretched across the intersection. Pushing through, he realized the north side of the street was likewise occupied: people of all ages, dressed mostly in black, as far as the eye could see. He crossed over to that side and shouldered his way through the crowd to a corner, where several young men in white shirts and ties and black leather jackets were grouped around a café that vended coffee and pastries on the sidewalk. The sound of slow drums and brass instruments carried on the cold spring air, and a wave of anticipation ran through the crowd. Omar remembered, only then, that today was Good Friday – this, of course, was a Good Friday procession, mustered from a dozen congregations throughout the city. He bought a hot coffee in a Styrofoam cup and stood to one side of the café. The young men, he noticed, were sleek and handsome, patently Italian and attired in outfits as appropriate for a Saturday night date as for a Sunday mass. When three leggy girls teetered by on black heels, in tiny black skirts, the men fell silent and tracked the girls' provocative progress over their shoulders and refrained from uttering the usual gallantries. Now and again, one recognized a female cousin or school friend and called out, "Gabriella! Hey, Happy Easter! You going over to Sammie's later?" And Omar felt exalted and lost, simultaneously high and sweetly desolated, for he was strictly a spectator, yet as hungry as the next man for blessing.

He moved away from the café and planted himself behind a youngish family with a baby in arms and a toddler on the ground, flanked on either side by somber older men in severe and well-worn suits, brimmed hats in their hands. The music grew louder, a hush fell upon the crowd. Now Omar could hear it clearly, a brass band playing lugubrious but heartfelt hymns in a slow, funereal cadence. Through the bodies Omar glimpsed altar boys carrying banners, priests in vestments swinging censers, young girls in robes and more priests marching gravely, their stern clean faces staring straight ahead. A sort of religious marching band materialized in front of him and the sound of trumpets and clarinets and sanctified euphoniums rose with the incense. The music reminded him of New Orleans funeral music, minus the swing. Listening hard, he could almost hear "St. James Infirmary" trying to break through the Latinate densities. But it was wonderful to him, it was real, and when he lifted his eyes he saw white clouds of incense weaving over his street on slow spirals, around the high street sign and down toward Carrie's house, then toward his own. She'd be in some bar or bistro across town, but if she were home, if she stepped onto her porch right now, she'd breathe the incense and hear the slow cadence of mysterious hymns, hymns singing the reality of death, the hope of resurrection. If the reality of death were not in this parade it would be a sham and distasteful, but death was present and strangely honoured and as the stations of the cross went by, one by one, floating above the crowds, Omar addressed his dead parents, or tried to, tried to summon the love or the feeling of love he had known for them.

The crowd tightened and pushed closer to the street. A child was hoisted up on his father's shoulders. In the gap between heads, Omar glimpsed clean-shaven, grim-faced Roman soldiery on horseback. The snorting horses made a thrilling sound in the raw air. In the ancient world, Omar mused, horses and music were the two essences of power. Every public display of secular power contained both.

Then, as the third brace of riders passed, he realized they were young women. The Roman soldiers were athletic young women in plastic helmets and plastic breastplates and short leather kilts.

A particular silence, genuinely grieved, swept the crowd: presently, a wiry Jesus in sandals and a robe plodded by under the weight of his cross. A Roman soldier – this one male – snapped a whip at the back of his legs and shouted at him to keep up the pace. Just to Omar's left a small girl began to whimper. An older man – her uncle or grandfather – promised her a pastry and led her away by the hand while people glanced at each other and smiled.

The last stage of the procession contained nothing more than an aggregate of the devout and penitent: fifty or sixty older, plainly dressed parishioners, mostly women, walking slowly, some clasping rosaries, with heads down as the music wavered in front of them. Omar heard someone at the corner call out, "Hey, Mario! There goes your old lady!" Someone else laughed, but a respectful silence ensued, as though a serious elder had successfully reprimanded the café swains.

He waited until the procession passed and the crowd began to break and move. A holiday gaiety now filled the street. People pushed around him, but he lingered and stared at the sign where College met his street, which had been blessed with music, touched by eternity.

φ

On Saturday, Carrie telephoned to ask if Omar would come to Easter dinner the next evening with her family and some people from her brother's office. Surprised, Omar said he would. "Just bring a bottle of wine," she said. The conversation was perfunctory, and it wasn't until he plunged into the crowd at the liquor store that he considered how short the notice had been, how likely it was that she'd first asked someone else who'd since cancelled. On the other hand, she was exactly the sort who'd play it cool with any man – and, more important, with herself. It was entirely in her character to wait until the last minute in a kind of over-deliberate casualness.

Escaping the chaotic store with his bottle, Omar rapped his forehead lightly with his knuckles. These were idiot worries that ate into his mental focus and muddled the work. He banished them from consciousness and spent the rest of the day anchored to his desk.

Nevertheless, in the morning, Easter morning, he rose earlier than usual and hurried down to the little Korean grocery that sold flowers. He came back with an exotic mass of pale pink lilies for Paulette, who would no doubt be responsible for the better part of the dinner's preparation, and three long-stemmed roses for Carrie. As the sun set on his street, he shaved and showered and put on a clean shirt and a sports jacket. As he walked in the newly fallen dark to Carrie's house, the wrapped flowers cradled in one arm, the bagged wine bottle in the other, he had the sense of doing things right for a change, of being in harmony with the holiday, the social order, and the natural world. He began to wonder if all winter he'd been too attuned to the ultimate music in his heart, too fascinated with that slow, inevitable current that ran toward oblivion. Now, the music abated, and the air he breathed welcomed him into a different season. As he walked he felt courtly and alive, as if he were doing what humans had done for centuries, but he was making it new, reinventing it without quite knowing how, or even exactly what it was. He looked up at the trees, glanced around at the small raised rectangles of lawns. They seemed stunned by the long winter; stunned, but slowly waking, as if they were blinking at him, as if they dimly registered his passing figure and took hope from him, as he took it from them.

At the door, Carrie greeted him and accepted the flowers and wine with a constricted smile, a blank and preoccupied light on her brow. She wore a blue flower-print dress with tiny sleeves like epaulettes sculpted at the shoulder, a spring dress that swished at her knees as she strode toward the kitchen. He followed her and asked if he might help with anything: Carrie said no, have a seat, she'd make him a drink. He sat at the little Formica table while Sam, the elongated Abyssinian cat, stretched around his ankles, jumped to his lap, and flowed back to the floor again. Carrie glanced meaningfully at the cat while she made Omar's martini. She seemed to want to do this for him, to prepare and serve it. Yet her air was distant, her movements were mechanical. As she mixed the drink, she told him she'd tended bar in New York back when; she told him about her dicey neighbourhood – now utterly safe – and how her luck and patience had finally run out, a slightly unhappier version of the story she'd told him before. As she set the chilled, thin-stemmed glass on the table and peeled a perfect lemon twist into it, she described the day she flew out of La Guardia, taking nothing but her violin, her beloved cat, Miles, and one enormous bag. Omar saw her then, the proud and poignant figure she cut, her chin defiantly lifted as she gripped the violin case in one hand, the travelling-cage in the other. He heard the bright way she spoke to the clerks and stewards and drivers who filled that fateful day, the hint of panic behind her voice. He saw and heard as if he'd been waiting at the same gate of the airport, as if he'd been seated just across the aisle in the airplane. And sitting there in her mother's kitchen with a perfect drink in his hand, he saw her on a clear summer twilight, arriving at the curb with her cases, the cat and the violin and the bag that contained the best-loved artifacts from the life she'd just abandoned. He had abandoned several lives himself, and he easily envisioned her hailing a cab, climbing in with her baggage, the long blue car engaging the airport traffic and joining other cabs, and he seemed to hear Coltrane playing a few bittersweet notes of acceptance and loss, just a simple three-noted phrase that hovered in the summer twilight.

Louise leaned in from the other room and said hello, peering through the reading glasses low on her nose. She had a glass of wine in her hand, lifted it and said, "Happy Easter, Omar." Then she went back to the other room. Omar gulped his martini and asked Carrie what had become of her cat.

She stood at the sink and grimaced.

"He got run over by a car," she said, "just out front. I keep a picture of him in my locket." She opened the gold locket on the gold chain that hung to her chest. "That's Miles on one side," she said. "And that's my best friend, Sarah, on the other. Miles was Abyssinian, just like Sam."

Omar squinted at the tiny cat face on her bosom.

"Did you name him after Miles Davis?"

"Not really," she said. She snapped the locket shut before he got a good look at her human friend.

As he finished his drink Paulette came in wearing a black, sleeveless dress, her short dark hair still damp from the shower. She touched Carrie's shoulder and inspected the food on the counter. Omar stared at them. The room smelled of orchids and shampoo.

Omar took a breath. "You two look like a million bucks."

Both women glanced at him briefly and smiled.

He stood up, and for the third or fourth time offered to help.

They told him to sit. Paulette opened the oven to examine the roast. Carrie made him another drink. She put it on the table beside him and said, "Excuse me," and vanished into the basement. Omar guessed she'd gone to check her telephone messages. Checking her messages seemed to be one of the organizing principles of her life.

While Paulette worked near the oven she asked him about his book. It occurred to Omar that Carrie never mentioned his writing, and now that he thought about it she never asked him about himself in any personal sense. He talked to Paulette about her job as a photo stylist, how she scoured the city to locate props and settings for commercial shoots. He found it easier to talk with Paulette than her sister-in-law and supposed there were conventional social reasons for this, that perhaps there were as many different kinds of rapport as there were people. He seemed to have a separate one with each of the women in this house.

Carrie reappeared in a different dress. This one darker, sleeveless like Paulette's, yet somehow sexier, more austere. On her, the austerity made it sexy. She looked, Omar thought, like the voluptuous heroine in a Victorian novel; whereas her sister-in-law was cool-looking and dark, a thin Sixties ideal of Frenchified modernity, Carrie was curvaceous and proud and white. Omar couldn't say if they were great friends, but they moved around each other in complementary orbits, as if each understood the appeal of the other. They bumped into each other and laughed; they traded asides in subdued, almost secretive voices. Omar realized his head was spinning. Two martinis on an empty stomach, a room full of rich scents. He placed his empty glass on the table and closed his eyes. He heard the cool click and scuff of their shoes on the tiled floor. For an instant, he felt everything: drenched in foolish joy, he looked up and grinned.

The doorbell rang and other guests arrived: Duncan's partner, Steve; his wife, whose name Omar promptly forgot, and their two-year-old daughter. The couple went upstairs to find Duncan, leaving the toddler under the eyes of Louise in the other room. Paulette took some food to the second floor, and Carrie and Omar were alone again. Carrie spooned gobs of mashed potatoes from a pot into a serving bowl. At the end of the hall, where it met the staircase, the slightly older Tyler tried to play with the toddler. Up and down the hall the tiny girl ran in her diaper, chasing Sam the cat, her mop of flaxen hair in her face. Tyler watched as if she were some magical creature, or perhaps a different species of cat. Sam, staying just beyond the younger child's grasp, slid behind Tyler's knees and crouched. The tot braked in front of him and pointed to where the cat sheltered. Tyler opened his mouth to speak; abruptly, the tiny girl unleashed an uppercut to his stomach, a solid punch that rocked him backward. The cat streaked up the stairs and Tyler gasped at thin air as the toddler disappeared into the front room. Tyler's eyes of bright, pained astonishment met Omar's, who could not help but laugh.

The wide eyes in the small, white face filled with tears. His mouth quivered, and he too fled up the stairs.

Omar laughed again. Carrie glared at him.

"She slugged him," Omar said, apologetically. "He's all right. He just didn't see it coming."

Carrie muttered and banged the spoon into the sink. He rose quickly and offered to carry the potato dish upstairs.

She thrust it at him.

"You can take this, too," she said, pushing a large salad bowl into his other hand.

φ

The meal was pleasant, with wine and laughter and roast lamb and the smell of flowers around the room. After they'd been seated at the table Omar realized that Carrie had changed her dress yet again. This one a looser, less severe robin's-egg blue that set off the darker blue of her eyes. She ate slowly, without interest; when someone spoke she held her fork and stared at the speaker as if he or she were rousing her from deep reveries that concerned no one in the room. Steve, the business partner, tried to stir things up by quizzing her about a former boyfriend.

"What happened to Phillip? I thought you were with Phillip? My God, Carrie, everyone knows that guy makes a killing in hedge funds. He probably has a million for every year he's been alive."

Carrie sniffed and forked some lettuce. "Hardly," she said.

"Well, the man drives a Porsche. That's all I can say."

Omar drank and smiled. When Steve asked him what line of work he was in, he mentioned his previous books, a biography of Brian Wilson and a history of church music in New Orleans.

"Omar publishes regularly in *Rolling Stone*," Louise added generously.

Steve made a face, as if impressed.

"Well, not regularly," Omar said. In fact, he'd been in that magazine twice. But he let it stand. With several glasses of wine in him, on top of two martinis, he felt inspired to talk about the book-in-progress, to spread his expertise a little.

Duncan asked if he had a publisher for it.

"Publisher and advance," Omar declared, somewhat sententiously.

"How much do they pay you for a book like that?" Steve asked.

Omar pursed his lips. The women studiously attacked their plates. He lifted his glass and mentioned a figure much higher than the amount he'd actually received.

"And you can live off that?" Steve asked.

His wife, a tall, sleepy-eyed woman sitting to Omar's right, turned and addressed him for the first time that evening: "I guess that means we could never get married, Omar. But I'll buy the drinks if you want to have an affair."

Her husband growled in mock outrage and Duncan said, "Steve once played drums with Chet Baker."

Omar looked around the table and realized that Duncan and Carrie and Steve were musicians: Duncan still played guitar in a band from time to time, and all of them knew how to make music. Omar wanted to ask Steve about the Chet Baker session, but suddenly he felt stupid. What did these guys care about books about music? They actually played. They knew how to live inside the musical moment, whereas Omar was outside, looking in, imagining what the moment meant.

"How did you get into writing about music?" Steve asked. He was drunk now, and good-naturedly putting Omar on the spot.

"I guess it's what you do when you love music but you have no musical talent." Omar raised and lowered his fork.

"There's something in music I try to describe," he said. "I never quite get it, but sometimes I come close. That's the challenge."

Louise, likewise deep in her cups, offered, "It's like trying to describe what it feels like to be alive."

Carrie, scowling slightly, said, "But that's not really what he does. He writes biographies and critiques and such."

All faces trained on Omar. He felt a light sweat on his brow.

"Well," he said, "it sounds pretty subjective, but I write about listening. Really, that's all I do. I listen, and I write about what I hear."

"You can fill a book with that?" Steve asked.

"Easily," Omar said. Then, assuming a different tone and expression: "Just recently I've been thinking how there's a vibration that jumps from song to song, an emotional groove you can trace backward and forward. There's a vibe you can follow from Phil Spector and The Ronettes to The Beach Boys and then to The Byrds. If you can follow that vibe you can pretty much understand the Sixties."

He smiled broadly at the staring faces.

"I guess it sounds flaky," he said, panicking a little. "Partly it's an arrangement thing that reflects the time when the music was made. The right people get together and take it out of the air and put it into sound. Producers and musicians, they make a moment. The guy who produced some vintage Coltrane also produced a record by Jack Kerouac."

"What did those two have in common?" Duncan asked.

"That's just it. They must have had something in common. In fact, both of them put out some of their best work the same year, 1957. A lot of people did their best work that year."

Omar grinned guiltily and raised his glass.

"That was good, Omar," Steve said. "That was good."

"But still not as good as money," his wife added.

"Speaking of money – " Duncan said, and the conversation turned back to real business between the other two men.

Almost as soon as the meal ended Steve and family took their leave. Omar helped Carrie take dishes downstairs. At one point, as he followed her through the hallway toward the kitchen, she stepped onto the heating grate with a serving dish in either hand and lingered, with the faintest musical sigh, while the rising heat billowed her dress about her knees, just enough to deliver Omar a luxuriant shock of recognition.

She stepped off the grate: he blinked, that ripple of wonder spreading through time, and followed her into the kitchen.

After the table had been cleared and the children put to bed, Omar joined the others as they settled into two big leather couches arranged around a low black table in the living room upstairs. Cigarettes were lit, wine glasses refilled, a general adult relaxation all around. Carrie sat beside Omar on one sofa. She flipped off her shoes and folded her legs beneath her. As her mother drank and chatted, Carrie stared abstractedly at the floor, as if working over some problem that might be the essential crisis of her life, or simply the logistical question of how she'd get across town the next day. Omar held his glass and listened. Every few minutes Carrie would rise, shift a hip to squeeze by him, bend and lift her brother's lit cigarette from the glass bowl where he'd placed it. Still inclined over the table, she'd exhale two or three languid smoke rings, replace the cigarette, and weave back to her place in the deep leather couch. Omar listened to the others talk back and forth and waited for the moment she'd rise again and reach for Duncan's cigarette. He supposed she was acting then, in the purest sense: that pure delight in gesture and simple props, play-acting as a girl does when she puts on lipstick or clip-on earrings. It pleased Omar to sit and nod at the others and contemplate the shape of Carrie's body as she leaned and reached, to observe the studied elegance of her fingers lightly and expertly appropriating the cigarette. The talk swirled around him, but he knew she was deep in her private moment, her personal movie, going through certain outward motions for their own sake, enjoying her own behaviour while her mind explored some distant scene, some lover or friend from last night or some other spring. And as Omar added his part to the conversation he felt himself involuntarily travelling with her into that private movie, if only as an extra, or an onlooker just outside of it.

"Well, tomorrow's a work day," Carrie said, and she yawned and rose.

Omar immediately put his drink on the table and said, "I really should go too."

She accompanied him down to the front door, yawned while he found his coat, smiled generically as he stepped outside. There he nearly tripped over Sam the cat, who materialized suddenly and weaved between his feet.

Omar caught himself and looked back at her, behind the inner glass door, where she gave no sign of noticing his near tumble, but merely gazed out at him, or into the night, with a distant and expressionless face.

He walked home thinking about that face and the way she had seemed to check out, to float away, during the after-dinner talk. For his part, he'd been pleased to be seated with the family, enjoying a civilized moment with civilized humans. But apparently Carrie stood outside of these moments; apparently her real interests and energies ranged out through the city restlessly, riding a perpetual tension of searching and waiting, waiting for that lucky door to open, for that tuxedoed knight that would deliver her, at last, to her rightful destiny.

He walked down the empty street thinking she had spoken scarcely a personal word to him after that initial conversation in the kitchen. She had, he thought, a kind of fate hanging over her, wrapped around her, a kind of fate or fatalism that told her with insistent whispers that her destiny lay elsewhere, with other people, that it would be final – perhaps beautiful, perhaps terrible – but it lay elsewhere with other people and no one here could join her or save her from it, because none of them were capable of imagining it.

If she were just a little smarter, he reasoned, she might see that he could imagine that other life. If she let herself, she might realize in him a rare compatriot, someone who got it, who could visualize the uneven trajectory of her life and, if nothing else, offer some comfort.

Approaching his house, he slowed and looked for the moon in the wavy blue clouds over the bare trees. These, he decided, were dumb and even dangerous thoughts, and he felt mild surprise at having them. Truth was, he and Carrie had little in common. Having been goaded and gnawed by that same sense of destiny postponed, he'd long ago scrapped it for a safer present-tense existence. Certain decisions he'd put off, all so that he might go on listening, tuning his ear to the airy void for that vibration he'd tried to describe at dinner, that moment within the moment that defined his world and his wonder and that nearly incomprehensible thing he loved.

Later, in bed, he turned out the light and told himself again that his interest in Carrie was futile. She was a grown woman who wore her chronic dissatisfaction like a Greek mask. His truth was not her truth. His solitude represented the opposite of her hungry search through the city for diversion, for love, for destiny's gift.

Omar rolled over, cleared his mind, and closed his eyes. He adjured himself not to lose his peace of mind, his precious sleep. The darkness around him was serene, was sweet, and he hugged it to himself as though it were his final meaning, his one true love.

φ

But in the morning he woke early again, just at dawn, alert and listening, as if someone had called his name. In his t-shirt and shorts he stepped out on the small, weathered deck and scanned the pale sky as if he expected to see bluebirds or bombers, omens of either extreme.

He leaned on the railing and peered across the rows of small, rectangular yards, other decks in uneven succession that stretched toward Carrie's house. Soon the small gardens would turn up flowers, the old Italian men would grow roses and vegetables, the Portuguese would water their vines for grapes late in the season. The chill, damp air made him shiver but he saw that the world was starting over again. He imagined himself sitting on Carrie's brother's deck in full summer, with potted flowers and citron candles, a cool drink in his hand. He imagined Paulette laughing at something he said; he saw the single cigarette Carrie placed beside her drink while the talk and laughter floated down over the neighbourhood gardens, into the gathering darkness, the purple city darkness that connected everything....

He crossed his arms and frowned. With dim uneasiness he recollected Carrie's coolness, his miscues and dumb bragging at the dinner table. God, what was he thinking? After everything in his life, it was a miracle that he still heard the music, that he could write about it. But wasn't it the same small miracle that allowed him to envision the warm summer's night where he sat with Carrie and her family on their deck, to hear the general music of the city and the night blending into each other?

A light rain fell on his neck and arms. He found himself mulling over the central dilemma of his Coltrane chapter. Omar knew the link between the man and the artist was obscured by Coltrane's movement from lyricism to innovation to lyricism again. It was this movement, Omar insisted, that defined his career: Coltrane the consummate artist who had to play all the notes and Coltrane the romanticist who could weave deep mystery and sorrow and loss into a concise, slow ballad minus any taint of sentimentality. Perhaps this movement, the ebb of lyricism toward the fury of creation and the flow back to a richer, more profound lyricism, was the movement of life itself. It was the movement every artist navigates while trying to render a mature statement, and it was the systole and diastole of the soul, perhaps the only dynamic toward transcendence that was available to humans. The visionary state meant nothing without the lyrical mode, and the lyrical became transcendentally informed by visionary intelligence.

Coltrane's whole career was inhale and exhale, back and forth between apocalyptic ecstasy and broken-hearted acceptance, until the music finally expelled him onto some kind of wondrous plateau that preceded the final knowledge and the inability of art to express it.

But on another level, this was also the story of how someone with imperfect or moderate talent raises his game, goes away and learns something rare that finds its way into technical forms. The story of how he breaks through to that place he has always yearned toward. Robert Johnson purportedly sold his soul to the devil down at the crossroads and came back to the city ready to play. Coltrane did it the other way. Gave his soul to God, and God have him the chance to hear, then play, something miraculous.

Omar stared out at the weathered sheds and wooden garages that lined the alley. Of course he couldn't write such stuff. Well, it was a hell of a lot more interesting than dissecting someone's talent. The night before, at Carrie's house, he'd denigrated his own. But he knew he was hoping that talent didn't tell the whole story. At least, it wasn't the story that primarily interested him.

He shook his head and shivered in the falling mist and thought about Carrie again. If their relation was fated, so be it. But he would not let will or want lead him farther onto that limb. Whatever was out there would have to come of its own accord. He would not trouble his will. Certainly she was not troubling hers. And yet something in what he'd been thinking about lyricism and knowledge and vision seemed to pertain to their relation. There was a connection there, he felt certain, though he couldn't put his finger on it.

A cheeky sparrow lighted on the wooden rail within three feet of him and shook its rain-wet feathers. Omar whistled a note and it cocked its head. For a moment the bird seemed on the verge of speech. Then Omar moved his foot and the sparrow vanished.

φ

On Thursday he finished his work in the afternoon and hiked a few blocks down College Street to the nearest Starbuck's, where he intended to write a few letters and listen to the jazz on the sound system. Tonier, trendier cafés lined the street, but he preferred the bland and unspecific congeniality of the chain shop, and he genuinely appreciated the piped music, usually jazz or old rhythm and blues, from compilations that often included his favourite songs and musicians. He liked the idea of the same music playing in almost identical shops across the continent. His counterpart in Boston or Cincinnati, in Portland or Vancouver, might be hearing the same song at the same moment. The blandness of the place gave him a sense of anonymous community, a sense entirely appropriate to the purposes and social limits of this phase of his life.

Today, however, the street out front was lined with big white Panavision trucks and klieg lights and sound equipment. Fat, coloured cables writhed down the sidewalks like pythons. They seemed to carry an almost visible hum of excitement that pre-empted whatever the street was usually about. Cops in orange vests routed the pedestrian traffic into the street, around a city bus parked in front of the restaurant beside the coffee shop. The crew seemed to be filming ordinary-looking extras getting on and off the bus. Technicians and caterers hovered about the storefronts. Soft sunshine warmed the afternoon. The smell of food and hot coffee filled the air. Omar made his way through the bustle and entered the shop from a side door. He bought a small coffee and sat near the front windows, pondering the activity on the street. Making movies, he supposed, had become the real work of the world, and all other endeavours stepped aside to accommodate this work. Civic authorities bent over backward to bring the industry into the city; the otherwise stern cop became a sort of errand boy for the movie machine. That machine was big and bright with money, but in the ultimate scheme, Omar asked himself, need he feel sheepish about his own work? In the end, had he any cause for shame?

He suffered a moment of doubt, like nausea.

Then his ear picked Thelonious Monk from the air, a slow meandering piano line that Omar could almost see weaving through the shop in opposition to the urgency and glamour outside. He sat back and listened while various extras and gofers came and went with tall paper cups of frothing caffeine; he considered how the music actually represented a mathematical purity, insouciance and order in the same shot, in complete opposition to the literal urgency on the other side of the glass. He had the notion that he was floating in a musical aquarium, looking out, except in this case reality was interior; it was in here, and the trucks and cameras and lights and flunkies feeding doughnuts to the stars outside were merely illusions fuelling illusions. Only the music was real, in denial of these. Each small, hard piano note was one more piece of a transcendent scaffolding that would safely uphold his life. He believed this, if only because of the urgency and empty seriousness of what he saw outside.

In this opposition of music and image, the inane tune became solidly present and the literal action and image were just brightly coloured gases, already gone.

Omar jotted words on the back of an envelope. He felt excited as he tried to write about the music flowing in the coffee shop. He felt certain that this was what the current scene boiled down to: real music in the air and the illusion of meaning on the street, the illusion of business beneath another of meaningless action.

Sitting there, listening, writing a sentence now and then, he felt sure that Monk had understood the uses of the will and the wonder of the moment. The musician and composer was always, but always, in touch with that wonder, had not muddled it with his will, and therefore had never lost the real world, though he disappeared inside himself at the end.

The doubt returned. On the street, the camera followed an attractive woman as she walked away from the bus, then threw her arms around a square-jawed man playing her lover. Omar felt a tug in his chest and warned himself that he was building cathedrals on the thinnest of musical lines. But Monk kept playing while the big lights glared and the cameras were dollied about, and he decided that he had been right, that in his world music contained and created the only sanity.

Later, when he stepped outside, the scene had been shot and only the long white vans and a few workers remained. The sidewalks funnelled their usual volume of swart old women and goateed students and overweight boys in backwards baseball caps. He had an idea that in the future almost everyone would be an actor – not in movies or plays, but employed by governments and corporations to walk up and down the streets and browse the malls like average citizens, because in the future there would be no average citizens and little, human moments would be impossible or rare. In the artificially becalmed future, actors would play normal people in a world bereft of normal people, they'd be hired to sit in restaurants or ride in cars simply to maintain a municipal calm in the same way steers were sent into arenas to soothe the agitated bull. People would be actors as they once had been farmers or shopkeepers – acting, however, not to create drama but to suppress it, to conjure the illusion of the old quotidian that once ordered the streets.

As he turned toward home, his eye caught on the tall, handsome figure of Harris leaning with folded arms against the phone booth on the corner. Harris didn't see him and gazed balefully at the cleanup crew packing away the film equipment.

Omar walked over and touched his shoulder.

Harris blinked and straightened.

"This kills me," he said. "I've seen movies made, I've been in movies, and still I can't understand why the average goon on the street doesn't murder every Hollywood type who takes over his neighbourhood."

Harris looked astonished and unhappy. Whereas Omar's take on all this was largely speculative, Harris was physically angry and incredulous. They began walking, away from the movie trucks. The late afternoon sun shone soft and yellow. Soon Harris was himself again.

"My friend Andrew has an opening of his paintings at the Addleman Gallery," he said. "Come along and I'll introduce you to some interesting people."

Omar thought that he had known enough interesting people for one lifetime.

"Sure," Omar said. "Sounds good."

Harris squinted at him as they walked.

"So what's up with the actress? Still seeing her?"

"Seeing her? Not exactly."

They walked and Harris waited for him to continue.

"To tell the truth," Omar said, "I'm not sure what's going on. The signals between us are rampant. But I can't read them. I think we're jamming each other."

Harris frowned, then laughed, lightly and bitterly.

"She's an actress, my man! Her signals don't mean a damn thing."

Omar let this sink in.

"I don't know," he said. "I can't read her. The only signal that comes through clearly is 'Run away!' But I like her. She's probably big trouble. But I like her."

As they strolled, Harris shrugged. He wore a chemical fibre jacket, a texture like rubber, the greenish colour of Lake Ontario in July.

"But she acts," Harris told him. "Why would you want to get involved with someone who needs to be told how to cross a room?"

Harris had used this line before, and Omar knew exactly what he meant by it.

Omar said, "She's such a good actor, or such a bad one, that I can't tell what she thinks, or what's more important, how she thinks."

"That's what I'm saying: she doesn't think. She reacts."

Omar recollected that Carrie had once asked him if he read many books. The question of how much he read seemed to trouble her.

"Sure," he said. "I wouldn't try to talk to her about Vorticism, but she isn't stupid. Her talents are dramatic. And she plays the violin."

Harris looked away and smiled.

"Don't get me wrong," Omar said. "I wouldn't go down that road even if she invited me. Which she hasn't. I don't even think she likes me particularly."

"But you're intrigued because she's beautiful."

Omar stared at the sidewalk and kept moving. He said, "Maybe, but it's not physical. The attraction is definitely not physical. As a matter of fact, she scares me a little. Physically." He thought another moment. "I'm interested," he said, "because she appears to be suffering."

They passed the pizzeria on the corner where the patio, open for the first time this season, sprouted blue umbrellas like tough city flowers. The faces beneath them wore sunglasses and relieved grins.

"Look at those jokers," Harris said. "Half of them already have tans! Just back from Antigua or Morocco. This place is more Hollywood than Hollywood because all of them are making believe it's Hollywood."

They crossed the street and suddenly came upon Carrie and Paulette and Ivy as they stepped out of a bakery. Carrie wore heavy sunglasses that accentuated a Joan Crawford rigidity. Paulette appeared preoccupied and not inclined to linger. Omar saw Carrie react to Harris – to his good looks and the news that he was peripherally in the same business. Her sudden, brilliant smile instantly banished the former coolness and a note entered her voice he hadn't heard before.

Omar said, "Harris is really a poet who does commercials to stay respectable."

Carrie said, "I wanted to be a writer before I ever thought of acting."

Omar couldn't recall hearing this before, and her bright, hopeful tone was new: a heavy wave of helplessness swamped him as he stood there.

Harris, on the other hand, was distant and refused to look at her. When Carrie asked him who his agent was he answered in such a low, indirect voice she had to ask him to repeat himself.

Paulette said she needed to get Ivy home, and when the light changed the trio crossed the street. Carrie looked back through her dark glasses and waved. She seemed to be telling Ivy to wave, too, but the small girl skipped forward and took her mother's hand.

"Speak of the devil," Harris said.

"Shoot, she was friendlier to you than she's ever been to me."

Harris made a sound of dismissal. "I keep telling you, boss. There's no point in trying to read her gestures. They don't signify."

They started to walk again.

In a different voice, Harris said, "She's beautiful though. I'll give you that." And Omar saw that he'd been affected. Recovering himself, Harris added, "But in that game they're a dime a dozen, those beauties. And her sister-in-law was far more attractive, if you ask me."

In three minutes, Harris had already gotten his mind around Carrie's presence. Already he'd categorized it.

"They're a dime a dozen, but I can see you're stuck on this one."

"Stuck? I told you, the signs are all bad or indecipherable. And I'm too old to ignore the signs."

"Lucky for you. Believe me."

They stopped at the pole where Harris had chained his bike. He unlocked it and climbed on and shook Omar's hand.

"How old are you, Harris?"

Harris looked out at the traffic and back at Omar.

"Thirty-eight."

"Same age as Carrie. Same as Paulette. Everyone I know is thirty-eight."

Harris said, "More people born in 1961 than any other year in history."

It was exactly the sort of fact he'd have at his fingertips.

Harris shook Omar's hand again; then he pedalled away into the flow of traffic. The sun was still warm, and Omar couldn't stop himself from imagining what summer might be like, in the right frame of mind, with the right company.

φ

In the following days Omar felt his concentration unravel slightly at the edges. He put in long hours at his desk, but at odd moments he looked up, his mind blank but expectant, clouded by the faintest doubt. In those moments he felt lost, he knew he was lost, his life had been wasted in the pursuit of some quietude he mistook for a higher truth. His book was just one more castle in the air, one more cockamamie invention the world did not require. From experience he knew that these were the times to work harder, to use mechanical momentum, in the absence of anything better, to keep putting words on paper. But mid-sentence his hand would stop, a pastel fog would envelop his brain, and he would have to rise and make coffee or stand on his deck for a while before he could take up the pen again. On bad days, as he stood looking at the blue horizon, an awful clarity descended and he saw the futility of his book; he realized that the thing he was trying to express, the continuity he strove to render verbally, was beyond him. A master's degree in musicology and years of listening did not qualify him to find God in jazz music, or anywhere else for that matter. The wonder of his quiet street was aesthetic, not metaphysical, and simple need and appetite formed the basis of his most acute perceptions. On the worst days, he couldn't even remember his thesis, he couldn't see the point he'd been trying to get at for several hundred pages.

Then, one Sunday afternoon as Omar came through the tunnel at the Queen's Park subway station, he heard the awkward but resonant phrases of "My Favourite Things" on a tenor saxophone, and as he turned toward the northwest exit he saw the musician, a man somewhat older than himself, standing near the stairs in a splash of yellow sunlight from the street, and the cloud of distraction vanished and he knew exactly what his book must be about. As he emerged onto College Street his logic and motivation came back as clear as daylight. He guessed his doubt had been attributable to being so close to finishing the project. By the fall he'd have a solid first draft. One last big push would do it. Nothing must deter him. His time, his peace of mind, were like gold. He must not give them away. And so he worked on, satisfied with the progress of his days.

One afternoon, while he was deep in his manuscript, the phone rang and he grabbed it, annoyed at being disturbed.

The voice in the receiver was harsh, garbled, like an angry old Chinese woman scolding her neglectful offspring.

When he could break in, Omar said, "You have the wrong number – " But as he started to hang up, another voice came through and he pressed the receiver to his ear again. "It's me. It's Carrie," she said.

"Carrie?"

"Sorry about that. Sometimes I go into voices, especially when I'm stressed."

He heard the rush of city traffic, horns and engines, the dull roar of the real world she was calling from.

"I'm downtown," she said. "I only have a minute before an audition. This is a callback and I have my fingers crossed." A pause. "What are you doing?"

"Same old, same old," he told her. "Trying to work."

There was another pause in which Omar heard the vital din of the city funnel through the phone, as if particles of pure urban energy were filling his upper brain.

"I've been wondering about you," she said. Omar waited. "What a day," she continued, speaking faster again. "I was late this morning for my audition for this headache commercial. Now I have to catch a cab for the east end." The great world roared in the receiver like the sea in a shell. "God, I get so tired," she said. "I get so tired I could just lie down and weep."

She laughed, a short, guttural sound. Omar listened to the city around her.

"There go three red cars in a row," she said. Suddenly a clatter, the sound sucked inside out.

Her voice came back: "I dropped the phone."

Omar saw her fumbling in the booth on the busy street, a small oasis in her frantic day. He saw the sun blazing on the sidewalk, the cars full of blunt male faces turning to gawk at the striking redhead in the booth; he felt the hot wind of commerce and sexuality blowing down the thoroughfare, Carrie in the thick of it.

"I get so damn tired," she said again. Then: "God, you don't know me! You don't know what it takes for me to stay sane."

Her voice held a sort of bright panic, or even exhilaration, he'd not heard before.

"You don't know me very well," she said in a rush. Omar gripped the phone and held on. "There goes another red car!" she said. "Can you believe it?"

Omar heard the car accelerate by the booth. He traced it into the city distance, into the ocean sound that surged around her. Suddenly he wanted to be there, out on that street, swimming through the warmth of the world with Carrie. That's what he heard above and below the dire whimsy in her voice – the real, wide world resonating through the instrument in his fist.

"I'd like to get together," she said. "But gosh, I'm so frantic I could weep. I swear, I could just lie down and weep."

"Better not," Omar said. "Better stay upright."

"Upright," she repeated. "Upright. Right!" Another pause full of gritty wind and traffic.

"Call me when you have time," Omar said.

"I will. I will."

He pressed the phone closer to hear the world and Carrie in it.

"Okay," she said. "I guess we'll talk later, then."

"Okay. Talk to you later."

"Okay. Bye. We'll talk soon. Bye."

The phone clattered to its hook and the line went dead. Omar hung up and stood beside the telephone, his heart beating fast. She had tried to tell him something the only way she could – on the run, between auditions, from the anonymity of the busy street where she did not have to order or edit her thoughts. This was how she told her stories – in the gaps of consciousness, against a wall of hot sound that somehow deflected their direness and ultimate meaning.

But how that vast, vibrating world came through with her words! The vast world he had denied so that his work might get done. How wide and mysterious and inviting – God, he'd forgotten the sound of it, the size of it, the way a human spirit had to swim against it, through it, every living day.

He drifted out to his balcony, where the blue sky bore down on the backyards and wash lines and old houses in a row on the next street. The splintery grey railing felt warm under his hands. Soon he'd be able to sit here and take the sun. He looked toward Carrie's house, that dream of summer drinks and laughter returning, as if he could hear himself talking happily with her family in the very near future, as if the future itself existed a dozen houses down his street, and all he had to do was step out his front door and walk there and the lush life of summer would be his, like spirits in a cup, and he would be in it like the tiny light of an airplane or satellite blinking in the wide midnight sky. His life would be vast and richly particular in one stroke. If he held Carrie's voice in his brain, the voice that came on the wind through the telephone, he could imagine all this.

φ

In the evening, to Omar's surprise, she phoned again. She seemed to be asking him to see a film with her at the art museum tomorrow night, but Omar couldn't tell if she really meant to go or not. It was a different voice from the one he'd heard that afternoon.

"You sound calmer," he said.

She seemed to consider this.

"I know what you're getting at," she said.

He hadn't meant to make her self-conscious. Indeed, he hoped she'd talk that way again. It seemed like an invitation into her life, that sort of talk, and at least a part of him wanted to accept it.

"Well, I'd like to see that movie," he said.

"I really shouldn't go out again. I've been out every night this week. But it's a wonderful Preston Sturges film. Sometimes I think you sound like someone in his films. You use those old American expressions. Anyhow, they're running all this week."

Omar listened so hard he couldn't hear what she was telling him.

"Well, if you feel up to it, call me back. Give me a call when you're feeling fit."

A brief, irritated silence.

"I think I want to go. Don't you? I'll feel okay by tomorrow night."

Omar laughed, but only silence on the other end.

"All right," he said. "Tomorrow night."

They worked it out. He'd meet her at the museum café at seven. She hung up and he tapped his head with the eraser end of a new pencil. God, this wasn't easy. This did not feel like fate. What made him think he was destined to know a woman whose speech was so oblique?

And yet, for the rest of the evening he felt in high spirits, relaxed. He still believed something bigger had them in hand. He was almost certain it wasn't his will. Perhaps it was hers. But he felt it was something else, outside of them. Something larger than desire or need or social attraction. But what else was there? That's what made it interesting. That something else. He would risk his precious equilibrium for nothing less.

φ

The days were getting longer. As Omar walked to the trolley stop on Dundas he noted the thin evening sunshine that slanted across the dingy street. Again he anticipated the season to come, ripe with pleasures and scents and companionship. A season worth living for. As he waited for the car he had the idea he might be confusing two separate seasons: the first proceeded from his private sense of wonder, the fascination with the evidence of his senses, the way the sky and light and the endlessly varied earthly surfaces opened to their loving penetration. The other season involved a world more urgent and social and literal, a world he might explore with Carrie. She might be the key to this second world he fondly dreamed of and undoubtedly needed. It was her world, or the world that came through the moving prism of her character.

He argued with himself that no matter how dangerous or deluded this sounded he needed to ease himself away from the fascination of his private wonder. This wonder fuelled his work, but it also seemed increasingly to impel a darkening current that beckoned like rapture of the deep. Ultimately, it moved away from that other season, that very human season of Carrie singing to him. Until recently, he'd forgotten the sound of such singing. Was it a siren song that would draw him back onto the rocks of his own flawed character? Or was it the token of his fulfilment as a social being?

In the middle distance the streetcar appeared around the bend, shuddering closer with ponderous inevitability. On it came with that familiar grinding sound; the electrical pole on the top of the car traced one line across the intersection through a maze of others with a static crackle and pop; blue sparks fell heavily above hurrying pedestrians. Omar felt light on his feet and larksome, ready to meet Carrie down the line. Perhaps he would persuade her to finish the story she had tried to tell him from the phone booth on the previous afternoon.

The streetcar stopped reluctantly; the doors flipped open and the driver glanced down indifferently, like the pilot of some netherworld ferry. Omar clambered up the steps and once again the car began to move.

φ

From the street he saw Carrie waiting inside the museum café. She looked up from her table behind the bank of plate glass and waved. She wore stylish tortoiseshell glasses Omar had not seen before. He waved and went inside.

At his approach, she dropped her pencil: she'd been sketching in a bound pad. Omar drew a chair and sat down on the other side of the small table. She suggested he get a coffee, since they had some time before the film. It had been a long time, maybe years, since he'd been in this place, and he wondered at the way particular city locales became emotional landmarks, the sites of especial defeats or triumphs. There was, he intuited, a neutrality here, a clean and social space adjoined to a great repository of culture. As a safe rendezvous, it made sense. Doubtlessly, there were many places in the city she could not visit without raising malign ghosts. This, he guessed, was not one of them.

Omar got his coffee and went back to the table. Carrie showed him the new pack of sketching pencils she'd purchased today; she pushed a coloured laser copy of a drawing across the table. It was Sam the cat, her own drawing, half cartoon, half heroic realism. Omar looked from Carrie to the drawing, to Carrie again. Her stare behind her glasses was both blank and acute, almost angry. Already he felt confused. The glasses, he decided, were a prop. She was using them for effect, and the effect in his case, intended or not, was to tilt him off-balance.

"I met an old friend today," Carrie said, speaking rapidly, "a man I haven't seen for years. We'd barely said hello when he lit into me for dropping him, for giving up on him way back when. I don't know why I just didn't walk away. People say the most awful things to me. He's rich now. Got into the antique business and now he drives one of those BMW sports cars."

The car and his wealth seemed to represent some kind of evidence or logic in the man's argument of being abused. It seemed to be something he, or she, could point at to prove she'd been wrong about him.

"I don't know what he's like now, but he used to have a horrible, nasty temper. He'd throw tantrums in public places. I don't think he's changed much."

Omar slid the drawing back to her and she fitted it carefully into a leather binder. She slipped the binder into her nylon backpack.

"Anyhow," she said, "the whole business upset me. I'm still rattled."

"Maybe we should get a drink. Must be some place around here we can get a drink."

But drinking, he thought, must be the constant fallback and standby in her life. He was annoyed that he couldn't come up with a better suggestion.

She frowned and glanced at her watch.

"The picture starts soon. Let's just sit here a while longer. I think I need to sit for a while."

She fidgeted with her glasses and told him how they didn't fit properly because of a defect in the bridge of her nose.

"You have the straightest nose I've ever seen," he said.

In fact, he'd been wondering if she'd had it fixed. It was oddly flattened from the bridge to the nostrils, very much like the elongated feline face she'd given Sam in her sketch.

"But there's this slight crook in it here," she said, touching it just below her eyes, pushing the glasses down. "I took them back to the optician three times and finally the woman snapped at me. She said the problem was my nose, not the glasses."

Omar looked at her strange, lovely face, the startlingly blue eyes behind the glasses. She met his gaze blankly and frowned.

"Didn't I see you wearing glasses once?'" she asked him. "Yeah, you walked by our house and you were wearing glasses."

"Probably. Sure, my eyes are screwy. I wear them to read and write. I should probably wear them all the time."

She furrowed her brow and stared at him.

"But can you see right now?"

He laughed. "Kind of. But now that you mention it, I almost wore them tonight. I thought maybe I'd need them for the movie."

She removed her glasses, put them in a small case and pushed them into her raincoat.

Suddenly Omar felt fatigued. What the hell was this kind of talk, anyway? She seemed to be fishing for some kind of confession.

Carrie glanced at her watch again.

"We might as well get our tickets," she said.

They went outside and around the building to a side entrance in the theater wing. Inside, the theater was rounded like a lecture hall, a venue for serious cinema-viewing. Indeed, many of the patrons looked like film teachers or critics but with a touch of Hollywood about them. Carrie and Omar found their seats and Carrie brought her glasses out again. She fiddled with them on her face, touching first one temple, then the other.

The lights went down, the screen filled with silvery light. The film was *The Lady Eve*, which starred a spunky, young Barbara Stanwyck and a handsomely woodenheaded Henry Fonda. Plainly they were destined for each other, but first they must complete the screwball plot that took them over many miles and months. There was an amusing scene with Henry and Barbara and a horse. To Omar, the horse's large angular head became the face of idiot fate, bumping the two humans together, nuzzling them apart. Omar glanced at Carrie, who absorbed the scene raptly through her new glasses with a rare, beaming grin. Her face seemed to throw off silver light, a reflection of the light bathing the screen. It was hard for him not to watch her watching the film.

When the lights came up the audience applauded and cheered politely. Omar filed out behind Carrie, following her to the exit. He had enjoyed the film and tried to say so, but she seemed to be willing him not to speak. It was the damnedest thing, but he distinctly felt an imposed silence. On the dark street, he zipped his jacket and smiled at her. The temperature had dropped; a winter bleakness had returned to the night-bound city. Carrie walked briskly, a step ahead of him. Every few yards Omar rushed to stay abreast.

"That film made me nostalgic for the great age of American train travel," he said. "You could board in New York and ride for days and days and eat well and sleep in your own berth and get off in a totally new climate."

Carrie strode purposefully, just ahead of him. He couldn't see her face clearly, but she seemed angry.

"What are you saying? Are you saying they didn't have great trains in Europe? Have you ever travelled by rail in Europe?"

He stared after her dramatically striding figure. The faintest of vapours blew over her shoulder as she spoke. They were wholly out of synch. It took an effort of will, but he tried to say something that made sense. She listened and sniffed, hurrying along the wet side streets.

Baffled, he touched her shoulder.

"I need a drink, Carrie. Where can we get a drink around here?"

She paused and considered.

"We can walk over to Queen Street. But I don't have any money."

"Never mind. It's on me. I need some alcohol."

Briefly, she scrutinized his face, as though she hadn't expected this from him.

"All right. This way," she said, and she turned sharply down another side street.

"Do you know where you are?" she asked him.

"Sort of," he said, labouring to keep pace.

"How long have you lived in the city?"

"Well, I've only been in the neighbourhood six or seven months."

"I thought you'd lived here a year or so."

"No, no, I'd only been here a few months when I met you."

She seemed to mull over this information as she walked on, always a half-step ahead of him. Whatever charm the night had held was bleeding into the darkness. He had no idea what was taking it.

As they entered the larger, brighter street he determined to tell her something about himself, something that would ease the tension and put them on a more natural footing.

Carrie led him to the orange-lit bar of an old pub with British beer on tap and American soul music pouring through a speaker in front of them. The bartender, who was probably also the owner or manager, was a slumped, benignly decayed Brit with several chins and a bleached-blond Seventies haircut. Carrie ordered pints of lager and commented on the old lamp behind the bar. Omar wondered if she was thinking of that former friend she'd bumped into earlier, the one who'd made a bundle in antiques. Despite his thirst, he drank slowly. They held their dimpled mugs and listened to the music.

"Etta James," Omar said. "On a given day, this song can make me weep."

Carrie stared at him. "Make you what?"

"Weep. Cry. It makes me teary."

She peered at him, then slowly turned her gaze to the line of bottles behind the bar.

His pint was empty, but he couldn't feel it. The alcohol wasn't kicking in. Carrie put out some fundamental uneasiness that killed the buzz. He felt unable to move or speak or even think.

In desperation, he said, "We need hard spirits! We need real liquor. It's on me. What'll you have? Brandy? Bourbon?" He flagged the bartender and ordered brandy for himself, a scotch for Carrie. "It got cold out there again," he said. "We need something for our blood."

The bartender set the drinks before them and spoke in thick Cockney. He wore a sequined vest and many rings, the perfect hybrid of Dickens and mod London with a splash of Vegas. Carrie asked him technical questions about the composition of the scotch. Omar noted her habit of speaking to everyone she met about that person's line of business or expertise. But she had yet to ask him anything about his book. Whether this omission signified lack of curiosity or shyness or self-absorption, he couldn't say. On the other hand, he hadn't exactly grilled her about her own work.

The liquor burned in his chest. He tried not to gulp it.

"Good," he said. "That's more like it."

"Don't get me started on the hard stuff," Carrie said. "My father drank himself to death. I guess I already told you that."

Omar pursed his lips and pressed his fingertips to the brandy glass. He knew from experience that the ghosts of bad fathers were almost insurmountable.

For no good reason, he blurted, "I find, now, that music is my main source of comfort in life. Like this, now, when it comes randomly and makes the moment. Or in a store or a moving car. Not a concert. Maybe a good club date. Serendipitous sound is what I like best."

Then he hit upon that thing he would tell about himself that would reveal an essence and clear the air between them.

He said, "Exactly one year ago I sold my computer and went down to New York and interviewed the widow of Charles Mingus for my book. What a woman. Can you imagine being married to Mingus? Then she took me to hear the Mingus Big Band play in a club. Did you ever go to 'The Fez'? What energy! The sound came at you in waves, like crazy circus music. It made my summer. It made my year."

Carrie looked at him.

"You sold your computer? How can you write without one?"

"What? I just write! The way it's been done for centuries."

She stared at him with that hard mixture of scepticism and blank incredulity.

"I almost sold my CD player, too. I think I hear music best when I get it randomly, when it's delivered by fate." He glanced at her and looked away. "Oh, I still play vinyl sometimes. I'll get the urge for a particular song and put it on the turntable. But that's almost ritual, like eating."

She kept staring at him and he could not, for the life of him, read that stare. Her opaque disapproval turned him inward again. He took a breath and gazed at his drink. An old R & B song came on with sad-sweet funky voices singing "Been so long..." slowly and mournfully, again and again. His throat constricted. His eyes misted over. Sheer failure brought him to the verge of tears.

"We need another drink," he said, and he signalled the bartender.

Well into her second scotch, Carrie said, "My friends say I should warn you about me."

He should have said, "Let's hear it." He should have said, "Go ahead and warn me." But he couldn't speak. Whether from fear of what she might reveal or frustration with the stifled vibe between them, he let a moment pass. Then another.

Carrie opened a compact and began to apply lipstick, glaring at herself in the tiny mirror.

While the music played, he lifted his glass and set it down on the bar with a clink.

"Someone," he said, "warned me about dating an actress."

She snapped the compact shut and faced him with freshly pinkened lips.

"I'd think you'd be intrigued enough to go along for the ride," she said.

He laughed. "I've been on that ride. It nearly killed me."

The hard blue of her eyes bore down on him.

"Hey, I'm sorry," he said. "I didn't mean it like that. We need one more round, don't we? A woman once told me I don't drink enough. She told me I'm much nicer when I'm drunk."

"It's probably fortunate that most of the time I can't afford to drink," Carrie said.

"Yes, but there's always a line of guys waiting to buy you one, right?"

She turned and stared at him again, her colour rising.

"You think that means anything? You think it's fun to walk into a bar and have twenty-year-old punks make noises at you?"

Omar said, "Oh, come on. Look at you. You spend hours each day on physical upkeep. That's exactly the reaction your commodifying for the camera. You can't have it both ways, Carrie."

She glared and worked her jaw. She knocked back her scotch. "Let me tell you something," she said. "I've been burned like everyone else. The day of my father's funeral my boyfriend dumped me."

"How old were you?"

"How old? Sixteen."

"Sixteen! Jesus, at sixteen it must have taken you about twenty minutes to find a new guy."

Her eyes blazed with a cold, dangerous light and he thought, What am I saying? Why am I talking like this?

Then he realized she was moving, she was standing and putting on her coat.

"Carrie," he said, twisting on the seat. "I'm sorry — "

She grabbed her pack and stormed toward the door.

He slapped cash on the counter, grabbed his jacket.

"Carrie — " He hurried after her, out of the pub, his breath making desperate plumes in the raw city darkness. She bent forward beneath her pack and plunged ahead.

"Listen to me," he said, trying to catch up. "I don't know why I said that! Really! God, I'm sorry — "

She stalked on, silent, but as he skipped forward he saw the faintest bitter smile on her face.

"I just blurt things out," he said. "I just want a reaction so I say dumb stuff."

"Satisfied?" she asked, hurrying on.

They walked on that way, Omar apologizing, trying to keep up, Carrie marching doggedly on with her hands locked on her pack straps, a bitter small rictus on her face.

"You think it's easy being me?" she said. "I just declared bankruptcy, did I tell you that? I try and try and the only roles I get are playing some bitch or space monster or nymphomaniac. A director suggested I get into porn, and you know what? I'm so damned sick of the straight world that I'm actually considering it! What do you think of that? That's how frustrated I am!"

She was almost screaming at him now as Omar hurried along beside her.

"God," she went on, "you have no idea the shit I go through every day. Every minute! You have no idea the crap I have to balance."

For a long minute they walked in silence. The air was cold but an earth-scented dampness carried portents of spring. Omar was trying to think of what he should say. He was trying to decide if Carrie was really angry, or if she was just acting, trying to make the night more interesting to herself. He was about to say as much when he heard a car horn in the city distance. Three notes falling softly in the layered darkness. His head came up and he listened for more.

"Did you hear that?" he asked Carrie.

"Hear what?"

"That horn. A car horn back there."

She broke stride and glanced over her shoulder at him.

"What about it?"

"It reminds me of something," he said, and he began to tell her about an epiphany he'd had, a sort of musical vision, years ago in New York, just as he stepped out of Penn Station at early twilight. He hadn't been in the city for over a year, and when he hit Seventh Avenue the energy and the heat met him like a familiar dream of summer. The concrete and asphalt seemed to tilt, and as the yellow cabs hovered and fled, he heard an unexpected triplet, a taxi horn tooting thrice, sadly, and thrice again, and he heard Coltrane playing "Lush Life" – those sad-sweet little phrases at the end of the vocal version, after Johnny Hartman sings. And what made this experience so remarkable was that he knew he'd heard those notes in exactly the way Coltrane had heard them. He knew that Coltrane had taken them from the street in the early evening mellowness of summer Manhattan, and he, Omar, had heard as Coltrane had heard, so that suddenly, there on the street, Omar understood that those three notes revealed not only Coltrane's musical genius but also his genius for loving the world, and that somehow they were the same. Somehow his musical genius flowed from his genius for love, and when Coltrane hit those last delicate phrases in "Lush Life" he was actually playing his torch song for the lost world, the actual world of sidewalks and sunshine, the sweet tangible world he knew he'd be leaving....

Suddenly they were on their street, standing in front of Omar's house. With her thumbs still hooked in her pack straps, Carrie stared at his face as if to see whether he actually meant anything he'd said.

"For heaven's sake," he laughed, looking away, "you might as well come up for a drink. You haven't seen my place yet. Come on up."

They stood on the sidewalk, gazing down the street toward Carrie's house. Omar could hear himself breathing. Then she said, "All right. Just one drink." Her voice and demeanour had changed again. In the sudden quiet of the house, as she climbed the stairs beside him, she tried to explain something, the reasons for her behaviour, her anger, everything: "All my energy goes into staying sane, into doing everyday things that need to be done...."

This was the voice he'd heard on the telephone last week. He nodded as he climbed the stairs. They went inside and he turned on lights and said, "Let's see what's in my liquor cabinet."

She stood in the main room and looked around while he rummaged in the kitchen. The liquor cabinet consisted of a half-full bottle of vermouth and one small airline serving of Jack Daniels. He filled a shot glass with bourbon, poured a dash into a drinking glass and added water, and joined Carrie in the other room. He gave her the shot glass.

"Have you read all these books?" she asked him.

He laughed. Once before she'd asked him about his reading. It sounded like a movie question, a line he'd heard a hundred times in old Hollywood films, but he caught the serious cast of her face.

"I guess you have," she said. "I guess you read a lot."

She moved from room to room, examining his household wares and personal artifacts with bright eyes and furrowed brow. They hadn't taken their coats off; Omar made no move to remove his own. He had no sense of what impression his rooms and strange knick-knacks were making. Was this what she'd hoped to see?

Undoubtedly she had access to comfortable houses and swank lofts, the homes of directors and young business moguls on the rise. Omar stood behind her, now and then reaching to retrieve a dirty spoon or flick away a clump of dust.

"And you do all your writing in that one little room?"

"Pretty much," he said. "I don't need much space for what I do."

She looked at him, tossed off the bourbon, and handed him the glass.

"There may be a few drops left," he said.

When he returned she was investigating the bathroom. He heard a triumphant "Ha!" and she came out wearing an old, twisted pair of eyeglasses he'd left in there, the ones he wore exclusively for writing.

She looked around, blinking through the lenses.

"You haven't really seen things all night!"

Her own glasses she hadn't put on since the film.

She handed his to him and sat down on the edge of the battered sofa. He took the armchair beside it. Her hand drifted back and forth over the long greenish cushions.

"Not exactly soft, are they?"

He shrugged. "Nobody's complained until now."

She downed the last of the bourbon.

"I'll have one more and then I'll go."

He blinked at the empty shot glass in her hand.

"I don't have any more. That's all there is."

She set the glass on the floor.

"All right. I'm going."

In an instant she shouldered her pack and moved toward the door. He didn't urge her to linger, but followed her into the outer stairway.

"I'll walk you home," he said.

"No need. What can happen between your house and mine?"

He insisted, and they went down to the dark and empty street – their street – without speaking.

As they walked toward her house Omar thought how he passed it every day, and she passed his just as often. Physical proximity had seemed to connect them, and yet they lived such disparate lives. He couldn't figure it, but he had the feeling he'd squandered an opportunity that might not come again.

Halfway to her house, she said, "I have to be fresh for early work on Monday morning. I got this part on a sci-fi TV show. I play a Pentagon colonel who morphs into an alien. Or rather, other way around...."

She was thinking out loud. The night was over and she'd moved on to the next engagement.

They stopped at her house, the windows dark, the bright porch light left on for her. She turned quickly and took the steps to the narrow walkway that led to the porch. She turned again and hesitated, slightly above him.

"I guess I'll see you around," she said.

He reached out his hand. She looked at it, frowning. Quickly, he folded his arms, feeling like he'd run out of gestures.

"See you," she said blandly, already gone.

He stood there while the porch light went out and the house receded into darkness. Through the shadowy illumination from street lamps he looked up and down the street, as if he expected someone to step out of a corner of the night and explain it all to him.

Part III

Two days later, in the early afternoon, Harris phoned and asked Omar to join him on one of the recently opened patios on College Street. He found Harris waiting for him at a table near the street, the warming sun beaming down on his handsome head and grin. A dozen other patrons in warm jackets and sunglasses sat around him drinking beer in tall glasses. The beer shone golden in the sun and Omar felt an ache of hope and nostalgia and something else, something implied in the impossible promises of spring.

Harris shook his hand as he sat down and asked him how he'd been keeping. Omar hesitated and admitted to a certain listlessness.

"Uh oh," Harris said. "You been seeing the actress again?"

Omar gave him a general account of the weekend.

Harris laughed, "Sweet Jesus, will you never listen? This is the one area in which I speak with unequivocal authority. Ignore me on poetry and art and everything else, but for heaven's sake trust me when it comes to actors. Stay away from them!"

Omar listened glumly and watched the waitress move between tables.

"I know these people," Harris said. "They're nearly illiterate. They consume the Sunday papers with brunch like a hangover remedy, then nibble on *The New Yorker* all week and consider themselves well-read. Most of these cats haven't cracked a real book in years."

The waitress took Omar's order and disappeared inside.

He focused on Harris and spoke slowly: "She seemed different to me. It seemed like she needed me for something."

Harris gaped at him.

"Needed you? Sure she needed you. She needed you to indulge her bad moods and buy her cigarettes and liquor! Of course she needed you. Let me ask you, Omar, did she ever once show any real interest in you, or your work, or everyday life? Hey, I've been there, boss. I've tangoed with that tribe. You're falling for a series of gestures, tricks of the trade."

"I guess," Omar said.

"You guess. I know."

"Maybe that's true," Omar said. "But I had the feeling she needed me in some way she wasn't consciously aware of. Not consciously. Maybe it was all in my head. But there was something beneath her manner. Maybe she's that way with everyone, but it was intense."

"Believe me," Harris said. "She is that way with everyone. She can't help herself."

The waitress came back with a coffee and placed it in front of Omar. He lifted the cup and stared at the passing traffic.

Harris went on: "I grant you, the best actors have a genius for living in the moment, for playing off of whatever's in front of them. But it don't signify. Today she's intense for you, tomorrow she's intense for someone else and she's forgotten your name. This is almost literally true."

Omar stared at the cars flashing in the sun. What Harris said made sense.

"You can't win at this game, squire. She's played it for years. You can't communicate because she's playing the game. It's all about gestures, not talk. You're a talk guy. She doesn't get it. She gets mad because you're not playing. Her old moves get thwarted because you're not playing, you're not acting, you really mean it. You don't seem to mean it, but you do, so she gets two signals that frustrate the piss out of her. It's hard to explain."

"But I think she thinks I'm being insincere."

"But of course! She only knows guys who hit on her and guys who don't. That's all she knows. Irony won't work. She doesn't know your sort."

Harris gulped his beer with self-satisfaction.

"In any case," he said, "it's all beside the point because you're not her physical type. She'd never sleep with you."

"Oh no?"

"No, she doesn't sleep with guys like you. You're not good-looking enough. These women have a professional standard. You genuinely interest her, but you don't pass the standard. She'd sleep with me, but the next day she'd find me boring. I'm being perfectly honest, boss. No, women like your friend Carrie spend their whole lives trying to have it both ways, trying to get Arthur Miller and Joltin' Joe in the same package. Then they feel cheated because the animal just doesn't exist."

Omar thought he knew what Harris meant, but it made him melancholy to hear it expressed with such suave confidence.

"Bottom line," Harris said. "No denying she's beautiful, in a spooky screwed-up sort of way. But I absolutely would not get involved with her. You yourself said she never smiles. Think about that."

Omar did. As signs went, it was not a good one. But his reaction cut both ways. On one hand, it was a warning. On the other, it caught his interest in a wholly natural way, the way the emerging sun and greening trees caught his interest. It did not depress him to think about her. But it was all too much, too complicated, too threatening to his delicate sense of wonder, even while it partook of that wonder. Here was Harris, handsome and afflicted with a high seriousness that neutralized his physical gifts, which he exploited to fortify his solitude and integrity. And here was Carrie, forever torn between her gifts and her temptations to exploit them; forever drawn toward the sources of her unhappiness. Only an idiot would try to mediate that conflict.

Omar said, "I know you're right about all this, but in a few years it'll mean something different to you. In a few years you'll see it's something you need to keep you interested in your own life. You don't care if it's delusion, so long as it keeps you connected to the planet."

Walking home, Omar considered what Harris had said. Of course, he'd been right about everything. Still, Omar's sense of fatedness persisted, beyond logic, but not wholly at odds with common sense and experience. He still felt that fatedness, and he trusted that feeling. He expected nothing material or sexual from it, but so long as he felt it he wouldn't fight it. When he could no longer feel it, he'd let it go. But likewise he would not muddy it with his will; he would not call Carrie or ask her out or in any way pursue a program. If he stepped into their street and met her, fine, he'd be honest about what he felt. But he wouldn't try. Trying, in his experience, led to tragedy.

He waited at the light and wondered at the traffic, all the people belted into individual vehicles rushing through the small urgencies of city life. How did they do it? How did they maintain interest and motivation? What drove them to office jobs and love affairs and school plays and workouts at the gym?

A small, black car like a mechanical beetle hovered at the curb, throbbing with the heavy bass line of interior music, then scooted around the corner scattering words through its open windows – *Alimony, alimony payin' your bills* – and suddenly Omar felt light as a feather, justified and glad, and he could not imagine anything that might prod him into that traffic other than his book, and certainly not day after day. If she asked him to, he might walk down his street to meet Carrie. That would be all right. But he could no more follow her into that mainstream than change the sound of his voice or the plangent shape of his face. Thank God he had his work, and his wonder. The rest was just noise, and perhaps for the first time in his life he truly believed it.

φ

He fell asleep on the couch and lay there dreamlessly into the evening. When he woke he felt tired but sane. He turned on lights around the apartment and made some soup. He took the soup mug back to the couch and turned on the television. The news went to commercial, and as he spooned the hot broth into his mouth he realized he was looking at Carrie, the same commercial that had been running for weeks. Carrie, in a tailored business suit, stepped into an elevator with two men, also impeccably dressed. The men looked mortified and ineffectual. Carrie, who undoubtedly had instructions to look the same, instead wore her trademark mask of opacity and disdain. Her eyes were lidded with contempt, brows arched, her haughty red mouth turned down in a faint scowl. Omar realized he'd seen the commercial more times than he'd actually been in her company, but it seemed that he was seeing her face clearly for the first time: the high, nearly unnatural curve of the cheekbones, the pronounced whiteness of skin, and above all the general effect of complicated unhappiness and superiority, a beauty so direly appealing that he groaned and splashed hot soup on his lap. He stared, even as the commercial vanished and the anchorwoman returned for the wrap-up.

Omar turned off the set and went to the kitchen to blot the soup from his pants. The impression of Carrie's unhappiness remained and he could not replace it with her real face, which he must have seen smile and laugh more than once. He recalled how deliberately upbeat she'd been on their first date, but he couldn't picture it in his mind. Perhaps he had never seen her real face. Perhaps she didn't have one. What was it she morphed into on the sci-fi series? Hers, he thought, was a beauty not suited to the camera after all: a beauty too terrible in its need, its pain, its superiority, to be selling long-distance plans or alien conspiracies or cleaning products. He could imagine the shrewder film and TV people glancing through her portfolio, remarking on her singular look but intuiting the grim intensity that would not sell the product or enhance the series.

All the same, Harris was right. She was working, acting, constantly. Playing the moment. She was a true artist, but an artist who must become the thing she created, a painter who became the canvas she painted. She didn't have the luxury of walking away from her creation. Harris had nailed it. It was a kind of curse, a form of purgatory, when the vocation you practiced became inseparable from who you were. But wasn't the same true and becoming truer about Omar himself?

His spirit sank under his speculations and he remembered her voice pouring through the phone, bringing with it the din of the great, seething world, the world he was slowly forsaking. Plainly, she craved that world and loved it with an appetite that might consume her. But her telephone voice, however desperate and ravening, had another voice inside or beside it that sang to him dreamily of sweeter worlds that might exist for the moment, the ephemeral moment that formed the basis of her art, not the commercials or the bad television but the real beauty of the real artist that lived beside the cynical commodity.

He went back to the darkened room and lay down on the couch again. What did any of it matter? He'd had his chance and, deliberately or not, he'd blown it. No doubt she had other men and similar dramas going on all over town. Men with cars and houses and real jobs. Omar couldn't compete. It was just that when he saw her on TV or the street he seemed to remember the existence of the larger world. He couldn't hold her image in his brain, but when he saw it he felt the hot wind and urgency of that lost world, as well as the poignant weight of her pain. Each made the other meaningful: she required the world's urgency to turn her pain into art; the world needed her beauty to bring men and women out of themselves, into the street. The world wasn't the world without it. She knew that, and that the world *owed* her just for being in it.

Lying in the darkened room he told himself, again, to forget it. And if he couldn't forget it to give his concern back to fate, which might or might not be done with Carrie and him. He reminded himself that he had just enough energy, just enough interest, to finish his book. The rest would have to take care of itself.

φ

While looking for stamps in a drawer, Omar came across a thin, silver pen that had belonged to his father. It was almost the only material trace of the man, other than a few snapshots and a wristwatch. The silver pen, the watch, and his mother's silver ring were all that remained of an entire world. Not counting an ex-wife who had utterly vanished, Omar had no family and there was nothing for him in the other places where he had lived. All he owned was the music and the wonder he still found in the world.

But gradually his mind drifted as he tried to write and he realized that he couldn't remember his father well, and what he recalled most vividly about his mother was her last years, spent in deep grief and heart-sickness for her lost husband. Omar had been with both parents at the very end; at their bedsides he'd seen the numbered moments of life fade from their bodies like a sigh. They were gone and in Omar only the colours of their grief and the ongoing shadow of their love for him remained. He stood at the window and stared out. Not recalling specifics, he supposed, was better than being haunted by particular acts of violence or violation, as Carrie seemed to be haunted. Yet, the blankness became melancholy. Summer's first bloom was imminent, the summer he had placed his bets on back in the winter. From where he stood he saw flower pots full of geraniums and hanging baskets that would soon burst into fuchsia; he saw freshly planted flower beds along the sidewalks and porch trellises that would be heavy with roses the next time he looked.

It struck him as wondrous and strange that summer should come again. When he died he'd leave behind even less than his parents had, fewer personal effects and none of that shadow, the blurred outline of love like the shadow thrown in a photograph his father had taken. Unless his book cast such a shadow from the wonder and effort and love he put into it. Was that possible? Did such things happen? Big hopes for pages that might never escape his desk drawer.

He reached for the telephone beside his desk, hesitated one moment, then lifted his hand and moved to the window again. He still felt blessed to have landed on this street, still believed that new blessings were coming. But he'd have to apply his spirit as well as his brain in order to survive. He'd have to find a clarity of heart that went beyond the benefits of solitude and hard work.

φ

Three mornings in a row he woke early, before dawn, feeling drugged and anxious. He worked sketchily at his desk, drifting in and out of focus. Slowly, like a circus strongman bending a band of steel, he forced his attention back to his book and the music. His ability to hear ideas in the music seemed to intensify with need and practice. Once, in the supermarket, an old Marvin Gaye song came down lithely and cool in the mentholated aisles, and he stood before the fresh vegetable bins with glistening eyes, following the sound into a realm where anything was possible. And at home, listening to Coltrane, he pursued a theory that divided the musician's career into three stages: a long bop apprenticeship with conventional lyrical detours that ended around 1961 with the first modal experiments. Then an all-important and unexpected transitional period of ballads and standards that in turn flowed into the final visionary mode. This second, transitional period – the one that immediately preceded and progressed naturally into *A Love Supreme* – fascinated Omar. Somehow, Coltrane had infused the ballads with a vast poignancy, an almost ghostly numbering of physical moments and earthly loves, fusing these in turn to faint, prescient strains of a higher love and spiritual transcendence. Omar tried to explain how each song, however familiar from sentimental misuse, became a moment that mediated loss and acceptance, that linked the past of particular loves and bodily affections to the acceptance of a solitary future with implied goodbyes to the unspeakably sweet world that had broken and healed the musician's heart.

The days collapsed into each other. Omar wondered at how easily he passed the time alone, how easily he filled his days with work and music. His eye rested on the telephone and he realized it hadn't rung in days; in that time, he hadn't spoken to another human being, not counting a casual exchange or two with store clerks, and suddenly he felt like a lost spirit, unattached and hovering. The feeling did not frighten him, but he knew he'd crossed a line. He was out there now. He felt ghostly but alive, like a sick man packed into a death canoe and set adrift on the ocean. His body was that barque set floating and his solitude was the ocean. Others had been there before him; he took solace in that, but still, this was new and unexpected. To jar himself awake he played *A Love Supreme* and read the liner notes again and again. He searched the declarative text for survival clues. When Coltrane wrote "I humbly asked to be given the means and privilege to make others happy through music," Omar understood that the musician had prayed for a kind of grace that might allow him to move beyond talent, beyond "creative expression," to a higher plane of communication. Omar tried to imagine how these notes read in the mid-Sixties. He imagined the record executives trying to talk Coltrane out of his written testimony, whispering among themselves that the words might blur the music. How close did they come to killing the package? He should make phone calls and find out.

But no misinterpreting the statement. The artist had *prayed* for help with his music. This man, in all ways tested as others were tested, had prayed to be allowed to go to the mountaintop, to be given first the knowledge of love and then the artistic means to share this knowledge through music. Omar felt his spirit droop: this was the way a prose writer thought, not a musician or a mystic. How could he write accurately about this man when he, Omar, could not think like him?

But he was getting closer. Surely he came a little closer each day just by listening to the music, by carving out the time and contemplation to get in there with Coltrane and explore the moment with his ears and his skin, as well as his brain. He knew enough to follow the technical changes and advances, but he must learn the metaphysic that lifted Coltrane's renditions and later compositions beyond mere form and technique. Omar had to believe that learning was possible. He had to believe that by listening, by living his own life in a certain way, he might be able to put what Coltrane had heard into words.

φ

Just at rush hour, when the traffic roared on College Street and pedestrians hurried homeward or on after-work errands, Omar stood in line in the Portuguese-Brazilian deli waiting to buy one of the barbecued chickens that roasted in rows on eight or nine spits in a flame oven behind the counter. The customers called out Portuguese witticisms to the sweating server as he shifted the spits over the gas fire. He shouted back in the same language, wiped his hands on his stained apron and everybody laughed. Omar stared out at the street and felt grateful he didn't know what they were saying. He liked their laughter, but he didn't need to know. Just like at home, when the downstairs tenants and various neighbours shouted back and forth: the fact he couldn't understand them served his purposes; he never lost his train of thought attending to what they said; their alien speech became an ambient sound like the distant streetcars or airplanes overhead. It gave him the comfort of human sound without the distress of meaning. In his work he peeled layers of meaning away from his material like onion skins; he didn't need to strain after it on the street. As he stood waiting, he wondered whether this reaction was healthy or unsound, a simple boon or a sign of his ever-deepening isolation.

He inhaled the aromatic heat that came off the oven and stared out at the dry pavements, the several trees on the verge of budding into leaves. He stared at the broad weathered sign on the Spiritualist Temple across the street. The text was New Testament: "God is spirit: and they that worship him must worship in spirit and truth." Omar wondered about the translation. Seemed to him the Spiritualists had omitted a few words from the quotation. Seemed to his memory that the word *him* had been left out after the second *worship*. And shouldn't it be God is *a* spirit? He'd have to look it up.

Omar mused on the text and thought about the liner notes to *A Love Supreme*. How plain and almost embarrassingly sincere. If they hadn't been backed up with brilliant music they'd have been excised long ago. But the package made an integrated statement. The entire artifact was a cultural landmark, unique in a time of increasing secular irony. In the new millennium, it might be viewed as a milestone in western consciousness, again like *Leaves of Grass* or William Blake's prints.

The harassed man behind the counter shouted and Omar blinked and said, "One chicken, one medium rice. Hot sauce on the chicken." Outside, on the wide sidewalk, he lingered in the waves of spicy warmth that flowed from the delicatessen; he breathed the soft breezes, the promising coolness of the sun-mellowed street. Again he read the sign above the rushing cars and vans and bicyclists: "God is spirit: and they that worship him must worship in spirit and truth."

What did that mean? What did it mean to worship in spirit?

He looked around and took a step. A short Italian woman walked toward him with her teenaged daughter. The woman, thick-limbed and vacant-eyed, wore a black kerchief around her head and a plain brown overcoat. The daughter, a good foot taller than her mother, sauntered coatless in a black sweater and tight jeans and high-heeled sneakers, just like the old Chuck Berry song. As she passed, she actually smiled at Omar and batted her big mascara-darkened eyes. Omar walked on, suddenly glad. The spring wind gusted in his face and he said, "Thank you, God," his heart overflowing. Just as suddenly he heard himself say, "I'm gonna die, I'm gonna die...," and the absolute knowledge sat implacable in his path and his eyes watered and he looked around at the world, the city street and the butcher shops and hair salons and the lowly humans pursuing their lives, and he knew that one day, perhaps soon, he must leave it all behind. He kept walking, overwhelmed with the clarity and realness of everything. A new season was coming, for sure, with secret revelations, and he didn't want to miss it. He wanted to stay. The sweet wind of destiny blew it ever closer, along with that final reckoning, but he must maintain course, keep his will free of selfish longing. He'd have that season, at least. He lifted his face and felt the westering sun kiss his forehead. *A little faith and I'll get there.* He repeated this to himself like a mantra as he walked home, racked by ultimacy, hungry for chicken.

φ

As if from the corner of his eye, Omar noted the warmer weather coming on. Overnight, literally, the trees outside his window burst into leaves and his golden sense of things seemed to rise slowly over the residential blocks. His own street was now a riot of flowers and fiercely green little lawns scrupulously attended by its Portuguese and Italian inhabitants. Gnarled old women in bandannas and long skirts swept the sidewalks. In the evenings, roly-poly boys and skinny little girls charged up and down the sidewalks on rollerblades or small silver scooters.

One night he went alone to a movie at the second-run theater on College Street. Maybe a dozen other viewers sat scattered in the vast darkness. Omar watched the film entranced, held by the light and sound; the storyline never penetrated his sensory attention. He could swear that he heard the finest auditory details in the film: the whistle of a faraway bird, a man's shoe coming down on pebbles, a woman's fingertips brushing the taut fabric on her hips. He heard it all. The movie let out just at midnight, and when he turned down his street he suddenly felt that he'd navigated into a separate dimension that existed outside of time and space, a dimension that was more real than the real places, like a dark and silent corridor between heaven and earth. From end to end, he saw no traffic, no pedestrians, only a few lights among the otherwise darkened rows of houses. He stopped, felt the current of otherness in his spine and skin, took another few steps and stopped again. Behind him, the grating rush of a streetcar shunted heavily into the night, already gone into the world he'd just left. Another one passed in the distance before him, a dim distant rush of colour and light into a realm he'd yet to penetrate. He walked on, noting the night-shrouded porches, the drawn shades of windows. A sense of mourning cloaked the street, a sedative of heavy, all-encompassing grief. He passed Carrie's house and paused to study the tiny lawn, the children's names in cement. He peered at two empty chairs on the porch and the dark windows behind them. The new leaves on the tall old maple tree seemed to respire sadly, somnolently, a secret whisper in the language of trees.

"Someone must have died," he thought. Then: "I have never been here before. I'll never come again."

He kept walking, looking around, listening: what a moon blazed down on his street, the trolleys running at either end and seemingly through time as well as space. Somehow he had wandered out of the world. Without knowing it, he'd turned left into a timelessness that pressed no future, that knew no past. He walked slowly toward his house, thinking, "This is my street, but everyone has gone. If I shouted, no one would answer. If I rang a bell, no person would appear." In the darkness of one porch stood a large, floral wreath upright on three metal legs. It looked official, funereal, like a memorial to souls lost at sea. He stared at the mass of blue and white blossoms and walked on. The darkness and silence were complete. He had taken a random turn that placed the rambunctious city before and behind him and he knew he'd been looking for this street for a long time, wanting it without quite realizing what it was, or how to find it.

Suddenly he was in front of his house. He went up through the dark staircase to his apartment. He lay down in the darkness and it was sweet to him. The darkness was like a liquor he craved. He wanted it to go on and on; he wanted to go deeper into it and deeper again. It was better than money or sex, because it was endless and final. But then he knew sleep had come, and with no desire in his heart, no sentences in his brain, he embraced it.

Most days, mid-afternoon, he'd leave his desk and wander the city streets while the verbal logic he'd worked all morning drained slowly from his nerves. The walking, he believed, was wholly necessary for decompression. If he walked far enough, if he kept his eyes and ears open, by evening he'd be empty and ready for those long, obliterating sleeps. On a Friday afternoon, after a mind-blunting week over the manuscript, Omar emerged from a bookstore on Bloor Street just as his old friend Megan flashed by in a neat little convertible with a tanned blond man one-handing the steering wheel. Megan's red hair caught the sun and garbled music spiralled from the open car as it accelerated through the yellow light and down the street. Omar stared after it and realized he hadn't talked to Megan in weeks. Standing there, he remembered he'd given up on her. They'd been friends for over ten years, but this spring he had decided to let her go. Deep in his self, almost unbeknownst to himself, he'd been dismayed by the way she went through men. Back in the winter, Omar had asked her if it didn't exhaust her to have a never-ending parade of males marching through her life. She had replied, "I need someone to adore me. So far, none of them have gotten it right." She'd given him a sly, sidelong stare and added, "We live in different worlds, Omar." At the time, he had laughed. But the sly look had stayed in his mind. And that word, *adore.*

He took his sunglasses from his jacket, put them on, and began walking slowly in an easterly direction.

There was something disturbing about her demand that the world produce an adoring lover. Of course, to varying degrees it was a demand that nearly everyone made. As he walked, he considered how Carrie and Megan belonged to the same club – a certain class of smart, good-looking women in their mid-to-late thirties with high expectations and a crisis approaching. The crisis wasn't gender-exclusive: he'd faced his five or six years ago. Carrie had taken the same route as Megan: testing and trying an endless supply of candidates, looking for someone to save her. Unlike the women, he'd had no choice but to step back and admit that what he called love was really something else, something desperate and self-serving. It sounded like rationalization, or cynicism, or even apathy, but Omar could honestly say he was happier now; at least he'd slowly, slowly revived his general delight in the world. Sometimes his solitude felt epic; sometimes it felt not only like a lifestyle but an accomplishment of endurance, a triumph of courage and endurance like climbing Everest or surviving weeks at sea in a raft. Other times it felt like a death warrant. He'd think – No one can live this alone for so long without floating off the planet. But he clung to his solitude to protect his delight, his wonder, and ultimately, what was left of his love. The important thing, he believed, was not to find another human being to save you, but to save your own capacity to love. That was it.

Omar raised his head and looked around. The sun leaned down on the city, the traffic; an unnameable excitement filled the streets. Could he blame Megan or Carrie for lusting after that excitement? Could he blame them for accepting the world's unsubtle invitations and blandishments? Was there anything other than this street, this moment, this Now? Essentially, that was what they were telling him: Carrie and Megan might insist they were searching for love, real love, but their actions declared that this was all there was – this moment and the sensation of this moment – and he was a fool to hold out for anything else.

A flutter of despair passed his heart. He breathed deep and remembered the dignity of Coltrane, the courage of all the wise ones who had preceded him. As he walked he felt unaccountably angry. Damn it, he loved this world, this shabby street and its mixed inhabitants. He loved this moment as much as the next person, as much or more than Carrie and Megan; he loved it with his mind and with a visceral ache he could scarcely articulate. He demanded no adoration, he only wanted to participate, to check in and out of a day like everyone else. Carrie had probably found him too careful, too ambivalent. Likewise, he'd misjudged her refractory coolness; undoubtedly she was like Megan, and if, on one of those early outings, he had dropped to his knees and declared adoration, she might have taken him.

Omar bumped into a burly businessman shouting into a cellphone and excused himself....

What nonsense. What idiocy. If he'd made a move back then, she'd have surely despised him. He and Carrie spoke different languages. Could there be two creatures more unlike under the sun?

Yet, he'd wanted it. No denying. He'd wanted some vividness, some living moments with the living woman.

He raised his head and tasted the new taint of air pollution: a faint smear of smog hung a hundred feet over the roaring thoroughfare. Somehow, this cheered him. Summer really was coming. It was almost here.

Omar walked in the surprising glare and heat until he spotted a magazine shop that looked dim and cool inside. At the door, he pocketed his sunglasses. As he perused the aisles he noted that nearly every periodical, whatever its topic or intent – whether it purported to be about travel or fashion or home improvement – advertised sexual fantasy or physical fitness. Moreover, those that dealt with fitness had less to do with general health than with buffing up for better sex! The magazine rows were like glossy platters of food and flesh and sunshine, all the ripe fruits of the moment within human reach. The magazines, bright with bodies and promises, looked good enough to eat. Or sleep with. They weren't for reading so much as pressing to your bosom, your face, for licking and inhaling and nibbling in the night. The magazines were sexier than sex.

He reeled slightly and stepped back. What a world. Jesus, he was sick of it. Sex should be outlawed, he thought. Only then would it stand a chance. Only then make a comeback. He easily foresaw a youth movement toward monasticism in the new century, a general turn toward some kind of sanctioned solitude, more romantic than religious in nature, simply to sidestep all the soul-numbing noise that killed sex at the source. A whole generation would have to go underground to get it back, to recover the always problematic integration of love and fantasy on which the West was founded.

Omar exited the shop and squinted in the hard, white light that came off the sidewalk. What were these thoughts? Was this adult wisdom or the reaction of a crank?

The heat and smog and noise gathered like a palpable cloud. These were real. Ultimately and in the moment, the world was nothing less, and again he comforted himself with these facts. So long as he kept his senses on what was real, he could trust himself.

Half-baffled, half-adamant, he walked on into the heart of the city, the buzzing midtown blocks, until his body was exhausted and his brain was blessedly bereft of anything that could truthfully be called a thought.

φ

Omar worked hard and well for long hours that blurred into days. He knew it was going well because good work always came with a certain physical strain. The symptoms were tentative sleep and mornings when he woke early, tense and alert, with trenchant phrases already forming at the front of his mind. Every fifth or sixth night he succumbed to the other exhaustion that carried him beyond rest, toward an oblivion that beckoned like a distant, fog-bound shore.

One morning, standing under the shower, he heard music in his apartment. It puzzled him, because he could have sworn he'd not left his stereo on. No, he knew it wasn't on, but he heard an eccentric bass line climbing and falling beyond the sheets of falling water, a musical progression both curious and sublime. He stood transfixed; he ought to get out and try to write it down on paper. He followed the musical line as it turned and dipped, as if sound, the essence of temporality, had become spatial; he saw it pivot and dip from room to room as he held his body taut beneath the water.

He turned the knob: the water and the music stopped. Silence. Of course. He laughed and knocked the water from his ears. He stepped out, grinned at himself in the steamy mirror and said, "You're into it now, Jack. You're definitely on the ride."

The next day, as he ran the vacuum cleaner around the living room, he heard a different sort of music – a bass flute that wove spirals on the kitchen ceiling just out of view. He even backed toward the kitchen with the vacuum roaring and leaned in, glancing upward, as if to surprise some mischievous ghost piping away up there.

Often, in his thin, nervous sleeps, permutations of this phantom music prodded him awake and back to his manuscript, as if he might translate the music, which was one kind of language, into the written word, the language he knew best. Though he was writing about John Coltrane's last days and final developments musically, Omar felt himself riding an alternative logic, just above or beside the material page.

All of this bode well, he believed, for the final product, but the process exacted a toll on his physical being. He slept less. He began taking vitamins and vitality tonics that he purchased in Chinatown. Every few days, for no good reason, he started to cry. The book got longer; the inward musical logics kept playing beside the sentences he strung across the page. One Friday afternoon his editor phoned to check on his progress: she put him on hold to take another call and suddenly Coltrane came over the wire playing "Welcome," a brief exaltation that felt like the musician greeting Omar at eternity's gate, all the grammar and syntax of earthly existence blown away in saxophone choruses that lifted Omar up on wings. When his editor came back on the line she had to say his name twice: he spoke quickly and hurried to his desk in order to write what he'd heard.

It all made sense. It all carried him closer to his goal, to finishing the book, but he still didn't know how it ended. To conclude with the man's death and a few falling bromides about his achievement – that had been done already. The whole enterprise required something beyond journalism or critical commentary. He knew he could do it if he stayed on the wave.

Peripherally, as he wrote toward the unknown end, he worried that this might be his last summer, his last summer on this sweet and mysterious earth. When he listened to "After the Rain" or "Wise One" or "Dear Lord," it seemed that Coltrane was telling him as much. And with an insight like a brilliant aside, he understood that the music and the musician were merely vehicles and scarcely more than ancillary to the meaning of the plane he'd entered. Though he worked in a bubble of eagerness and exhilaration, the sleeplessness and crying jags continued. Occasionally his hand shook as he held the pen thwartwise to the page in the typewriter. Fixing it there with sheer will, unable to make another word, he watched the pen's zigzags accrue like seismographic readings or musical scores for an instrument that had not yet been invented.

φ

On a brilliant Monday morning when the sun streamed gold and green into his study he left his desk and went to the window at the exact moment that Carrie walked by on the street's far sidewalk. In a glance, Omar perceived her downcast face, her blue-green plaid skirt and knee socks and navy blue blazer, a bag in either hand and a pack on her back – for all the world like a schoolgirl wandering home in a funk. Plainly she'd been out of town, was returning from a weekend in New York – somehow Omar felt this was the case – and her red hair, unruly and uncharacteristically curled, fell in her face. He thought he heard her loafers scuff the sun-whitened sidewalk, and he saw fate gathered over her, heavy fate attached to her, tilted just above like a negative halo. He stared after her figure as it diminished beyond the green boughs and golden light. His breath came in shallow stabs. He swung his gaze to the desk, littered with pages, where he'd been sitting minutes ago. The energy he'd been riding vanished into the morning, replaced by raw fear, as if something terrible were about to be revealed. He went into the other room and stood before the silent stereo. What had he seen just now? The actual woman, in and out of time: he'd seen the shape of her suffering, self-inflicted like a curse, the momentum of it, pushing her inevitably toward fantastic but predictable ends. He'd seen her acting out that inevitability, giving it narrative form and interest, even as it took her away from the things she loved. It was always a question of love with people like Carrie – and himself. Her declaration that she might as well do porn films flashed to mind; for all he knew she was making them; recalling her image just now he felt it was altogether possible. And at the bottom of that, a vague grief, for himself as well as Carrie. For they had arrived at similar moments in their personal destinies, moments that might decide everything, that might lock them into individual directions that would carry them to fulfilment or despair. He knew it sounded silly, or presumptuous, but just now they were poised on the critical moment that preceded ultimacy. He couldn't say what her options were, but his involved the book, getting it right, breaking through or settling for a higher grade of journalism. And something else. He couldn't name it, but he felt there was something else he ought to be considering, something that would determine the contour of the rest of his life.

He laughed aloud, then frowned. It occurred to him that this unnameable something else concerned Carrie. His imagination leaped and he saw that their individual fates were already cast; despite the appearance of choices and paths, if they pressed on alone their individual lives could only take inevitable directions. Very separate ways, his and hers. But he saw a wildly unlikely possibility of creating a third way between them. He saw this possibility as clearly as the light that filled his rooms, plain as a telegram sent from the ledge he and Carrie shared at this moment.

But what was he thinking? He scarcely knew the woman. Whatever he knew or thought he knew about Carrie was of no earthly use to either of them. Still, it seemed true that the wonder of love, the possibility that love generated and regenerated, proceeded from an unforeseen third way, where before there had only been the generally fated direction of each person's character. Again he wondered if this third way could also be fated or preordained.

He shook off his reverie and went back to his desk and worked through the day. But the image of Carrie striding homeward in her schoolgirl tartans, her face pouting downward and abstracted, stayed with him. It was permanent, he knew, in his mind's picture gallery. He had it forever, to forever puzzle its meaning, which might become clearer or darker as he and she surrendered gradually to their respective fates. And what could those fates be, he reasoned, but separate; she to be engulfed by the great frantic world, he to disappear into his work and solitude, which carried him like strange currents toward the future unknown.

The next morning Omar wrote until noon, scanned what he'd written, and threw it away. After a small lunch he walked into the city, the great blue sky above it like an ocean. His frustration and fatigue gradually lifted in the general clamour of the street. He felt the tug of excitement from the sprawling commercial avenues; he drifted beside big stores with immaculate interiors behind sheets of tinted glass. Then into the financial district, whose buildings were like towering dark crystals in a giant tuner, a huge radio that hummed with unnatural, all-encompassing urgency. The urgency was man-made and man-felt but unquestionably real, almost sexual in its apparent effect on the over-groomed men and women on the street. As Omar wandered this maze of concrete and glass he wondered how art ever got made, how music ever got played, how anyone ever got far enough away from this vibration of money-thrills to hear a tune or write a sentence. And yet, having lived so long in his own book, the nervous excitement of the street did not fail to touch him. The smell of money mingled with the scent of human intrigue, all the old distractions from death and consciousness, and he had the notion as he stood staring before the monolithic headquarters of an international bank that the money idea had become all-important precisely because of the inherent unhappiness in human beings. Not because people were born greedy or wanting, but because mostly they needed to forget, to climb out from under the weight of their own brains, and money – the making of it as much as the spending – made for a sanctioned diversion from the complicated and excruciating awareness of being alive. The people who made money, the ones he knew and knew of, were intelligent but uneasy, unable to sit still – marked less by avarice than by their inability to be alone.

As Omar was thinking in this way, the sexual tilt of the street levelled, the edge went out of the air. Just then, in the waning afternoon, he heard three taxicab notes, three F sharps in the early summer day, and he decided that this place was death, or the simulacrum of purgatory; not the vivid agony of hellfires but the flat air of perpetual sadness, the endless grey of regret and hearts drained of wonder. Here was the other side of lush life, the place where memory, like a pool of sunlight on a cloudy day, glowed briefly then bled away into the grey void. He heard the taxi horns again, but now he saw how the love and the memory of love was a finite substance that faded like daylight under the common duress of making a living and building a life.

An hour later, as he walked home, he passed a grimy bar. Music spilled through the open door, bouncing baritone sax riffs splashed in the littered street and Omar's spirit lifted. He stopped and smiled at Gerry Mulligan's happy tone, the undergraduate insouciance in what eternally young Mulligan was blowing. It would make another book, or at least an essay or chapter: Gerry Mulligan as the epitome of youthful zeal, the very sound of undergraduate glee from 1957, a sound so specific, that it conjured an exact picture of the boy strolling happily on campus, snapping his fingers to the muse that lived with him, the song of his joy that sounded a lot like "Disc Jockey Jump" or "Westwood Walk," which he alone heard in the sun-drenched morning air.

Omar coughed and looked around, back in the moment again. He uttered a short prayer of thanks that he did not work on those vast marbled boulevards of commerce. He decided that after all he was in a period of grace; whatever blunders or oversights he committed at this time would not be held against him. Whether this grace proceeded from attending the music or from thinking hard about things that were hard to think about, or both, he decided that he had indeed entered a rare and salubrious space.

"A grace period," he said, and he walked on, his mind liberated and mulling over the joyously inane facts that littered his past: a breakfast cereal he'd subsisted on in his teens; a brand of peanut butter with jam swirled through the jar; a particular pair of high-top sneakers from the summer of his seventh year. He recalled the summer and the sneakers precisely. His feet would never be that happy again.

He walked on in the rising heat. He thought of fruit-stripe chewing gum. Where had all the striped gum gone?

Some commotion behind him. Car horns dogging the near distance. Now voices.

"Omar!"

His head swivelled and he focused. At first he didn't recognize the car or the face in it or the voice.

"Omar! For heaven's sake — "

Pretty laughter, and then he knew the smiling woman behind the dark glasses in the car that cruised slowly beside him.

The car shot forward and snugged into a parking slot. Omar walked over to it. Paulette looked up at him, beaming, the sun making tiny fireballs on her glasses.

"We've been honking and calling you for half a block!"

Omar crouched beside the car and squinted. Ivy sat on the passenger side, waifish and wide-eyed, staring at him as if he were an exotic fish.

Paulette couldn't stop grinning.

"You were in outer space. You should have seen yourself."

Omar grinned back at her and focused on a point of light down the street. "Yes, I get a little spacey when I'm walking."

"We're on our way home. Do you want a lift?"

He opened the back door and climbed in behind Paulette. She signalled and scooted neatly into the traffic. Her bare arm reached and adjusted the rear-view. Ivy turned around to peer at him. He smiled and placed both hands on the curve of the seat. Tall, glossy shopping bags from stylish stores crowded the footwells and the space beside him. Scents of vanilla and cinnamon rose from them. He breathed deeply and relaxed. He still couldn't believe summer had come.

In a pleasantly modulated voice, Paulette spoke over her shoulder: "I had to take Ivy to the doctor. She's thrilled because she got out of school for the afternoon."

Omar sat back and enjoyed the air conditioning and the sound of Paulette's voice.

"When does summer vacation begin?"

Ivy looked around and held up two fingers.

"Two weeks," she said. "Actually, one week and three days."

She brushed a long strand of hair from her face and looked enough like her mother for Omar to imagine Paulette at that age, slightly introverted but shrewd, organizing the other girls and later, in adolescence, being cool but good with the books, too. In three or four years Ivy would be the beauty in the house, and he could imagine Carrie competing with the teenager, dispensing dating tips even as she undertook ever more urgent measures to mask her age.

Paulette said, "Why don't you stop by the house tomorrow night? Duncan doesn't work the next day and we thought we'd fire up the barbecue in the backyard if the weather holds."

"That would be nice," Omar said. But he wasn't sure. Carrie might not want him around. On the other hand, Paulette's invitation might be predicated on specific knowledge that Carrie wouldn't be in the house. It was complicated.

As if reading his thoughts, Paulette said, "What's the latest in the Carrie and Omar saga? Have you seen her lately?"

Omar guessed that Paulette knew pretty much everything about her sister-in-law's comings and goings. You couldn't hide much in that house.

"Not lately," he said, gazing out at the traffic.

"I don't want to give anything away," Paulette said, "but Carrie likes you, Omar. Of course, she'd like you better if you owned a car, but I think she likes you."

He thought he saw the heat coming off the other cars. In his youth, automobiles were green or orange or odd shades of blue. Now they were mostly grey or silver or black. There were white ones too, with occult medallions dangling from the rear-view, or small rectangular religious installations that looked like gilded tissue-boxes in the back windows. Perhaps they were just deodorizers.

Paulette turned to Ivy and poked her with an elbow.

"What do you think? Does Carrie like him?"

Ivy's reedy little voice blew back on the air-conditioning: "I think she likes him."

Omar glanced at Paulette's dark glasses in the mirror.

"Well, Carrie and I seem to argue a lot."

She steered smoothly around some stalled traffic and accelerated through the amber light.

"Oh, that's just her neurotic way of keeping you at a distance. Just assure her you're not romantically interested and everything will go okay."

Omar blinked and drew a breath. He kept his eyes on the storefronts and cars and pedestrians sliding past his window.

The car turned, abruptly leaving the glare and noise for the shaded cool of their street. It stopped in front of his house. Omar got out and ducked to thank Paulette. He noted that her hair and sleeveless top and dark glasses and sheeny pants matched the black finish of the idling car.

"See you soon," he said.

"Call us sometime," Paulette called brightly.

Omar stepped back and the car pulled away, rolling slowly through the patches of shadow and sunshine on their street, the street that he believed might save him.

Part IV

Omar had hoped he might finish a rough draft of the Coltrane section, and of the book, within the month, but the pages kept accumulating, the section grew longer, denser, like a fat wave rolling up to its peak. He had only the vaguest sense of calendar time: the days passed deep in the language wave while summer bloomed and the first real heat came down on the city like a dim, brutal glory. When he picked up the phone, he realized that he had a backlog of messages from Megan, his editor, and others. He pressed a button and discharged them into the void. All afternoon he tried to unravel a writing problem, picking at it, changing his mind, starting over. Just now Omar realized he needed to say more about certain sidemen who had played in the classic bands behind the musicians that his book featured. A radical oversight. He'd have to go back and remedy that. Looking through the stacked manuscript pages, some of them typed, most in raw longhand, made him seasick. He had to get out – out of this room, this house, if only for an hour or two.

As soon as he hit the sidewalk he felt better. When the book was done he'd start jogging or riding his bike again. The early evening sun came softly through the trees, the high and lush branches that arched over his street. His brain went back to the manuscript: strange how individuals in the landmark ensembles behind the greats were never as good when they cut solo albums. McCoy Tyner played pretty good piano on his own records, but given Coltrane's demands he shone, he nearly reinvented the keyboard as a rhythm instrument. And Charlie Rouse would always be known for his work with Monk, adding concise, somehow Japanese-sounding statements to the funny figures Monk added and subtracted at the piano. Who knows how anyone learns his craft, then transcends it? A man needs a rare set of conditions, Omar reflected, to lift himself into a new stratosphere, to transcend his puny talent. How rare were those conditions? Can an artist create them for himself or is it all chance? Fluke happenstance?

He walked up to a café on College Street and sat at the cool end of the bar and listened to the piped jazz, classic Blue Note stuff that made the place feel cooler, more alive. The bartender was a willowy young woman who greeted Omar by name and asked after his work: Lisa was another actor, maybe ten years younger than Carrie. She'd also spent a decade in New York, attended the same acting school just after Carrie had studied there; like Carrie, she'd worked that town with thousands of other actors, perhaps passing Carrie in audition lines. She'd relocated here last fall, about the same time Omar had moved to the neighbourhood.

Lisa stood behind the bar and sipped an iced tea and mused about the uphill struggle of her career: "I had to leave New York," she said. "I wasn't breaking through to the next level. You know what I mean?"

She served a man down the bar and returned.

"You know what, Omar? The acting business is breaking my heart."

He believed her, but she said it so prettily that he smiled and nodded and shrugged. She was a good enough bartender, quick and pleasant, but with a gossipy intimacy just beneath the professional veneer.

"One more, Omar?"

He furrowed his brow.

"How many have I had?"

She laughed melodiously and said, "Two. But stay and keep me company. I think Omar means One More."

She and Carrie, Omar considered, were very different sorts of actors. Carrie had a brooding and self-serious glamour, whereas Lisa was girlish and quirky, with a nervous sparkle that might or might not work on camera. He watched her make a cocktail in a nickelled shaker, the contents sliding in a smooth froth into the glass. The glass floated above the tables on a small tray as she moved toward the open front of the café. Omar drank his beer and absorbed the music. This was the way he liked to hear it now: randomly, in public spaces. From time to time he fired up his turntable at home and played some choice vinyl, but usually he trusted chance and circumstance to bring what they might. The hearing was purer, more spontaneous and meaningful: he actually heard the notes this way.

She came back with the tray under her arm and stood close to him. In a lowered monotone she said, "Omar, one of those guys I just served is a big TV producer. Bruno Hassenbach. Don't look! You must have heard of him."

Omar stared discreetly at his beer and shook his head.

"He produces *Shakers*. I'd kill to get a part on that show."

"*Shakers*? Not a religious drama, I take it."

"*You know!*" She spoke in urgent whispers. "It's kind of a soap opera about intrigues in a big financial office."

"Right."

"Now listen. When I take them the bill or another round, I want you to drift by on your way out and congratulate me on my role in the new Spike Lee movie."

He looked at her. "You were in a Spike Lee movie?"

"Not exactly. But just say you were impressed by my bit in it."

Omar sipped his beer and shook his head again.

"I can't do it," he said. "I would if I could, but I'd screw it up. I'd make fools of us."

She sighed and gave her bar rag a listless shake.

"All right, never mind," she said. She went back behind the counter. "You're right, he'd never buy it. Still, I have to do something...."

Omar stole a glance at the obese man in the Hawaiian shirt, who threw back his head and laughed at a crony's remark. What a life, Omar thought. What a life these women lead, plying the business so desperately with the best parts of their youth and hopefulness, offering their capacity for wonder to the machine. How terribly strange that the industry had infiltrated this heretofore dowdy northern town; how strange that this woman and Carrie had invested their best years in New York, gone to the same school, knocked on the same doors, then returned here with the remnant of that wonder like a favourite sweater packed in a travelling bag. Their experience, he supposed, was not uncommon, but it struck him as significant. He felt he had something rare to tell them, something that might shed a broad light on their frustrations, if only they would hear him. Sitting there with his beer, watching his bartender friend step up onto a chair to feed new CDs into the sound system, he felt that gem of knowledge on the tip of his tongue, ready to deliver it whole on the twilight city air that drifted through the café's open front. Then it vanished. The music came on, the same Marvin Gaye tune he'd heard in the supermarket a few days before – weeks ago, rather. He closed his eyes and tried to account for his time. His book was swallowing his life. Entire seasons were disappearing into a black hole that might not give anything back.

He looked up and felt the music on his skin like a fine, electric rain. This might be his last summer. His last summer on earth. All would be decided in the next few months.

He put his money on the bar and slid off the stool. As he walked out he passed the producer's table: Lisa was serving fresh drinks; for the briefest instant her panic-stricken eye caught his; he heard the producer announce jovially, "...they got married and he went straight to hell. Straight to hell...."

Then Omar was on the sidewalk, the music fading behind him in the nearly sweet evening air.

φ

The street surprised him with white light and noise, in full night-life mode. A soft blue darkness stood high above the city's glow. He walked the strip and turned down a side street between rows of handsome older houses beneath heavy murmuring trees. He peered up into their dense canopies and dimly perceived angels, the dark angels of humid summer nights. He walked until he was tired and then made his way back to College, where the bars and restaurants were quieter than they had been earlier, though they were still serving. When he turned down his street the silence intensified, the darkness thickened around the ghostly lamps, and again he had that feeling of having negotiated a secret place, a separate time in the night-filled universe. He passed the darkened houses, the now-still trees that seemed more like monuments than living things. He was about to judge himself absolutely alone in the world when he heard a voice and saw a flicker of candlelight from Carrie's porch.

"Omar?"

He crossed the street and came closer and recognized Carrie's mother sitting there, smoking a cigarette and nursing a drink.

"Come up and have a nightcap," she said.

He hesitated, looked up and down the street, then went up the walkway to the porch. Louise pushed a plastic chair toward him, then disappeared inside to make his drink. The screen door clicked softly behind her; he heard the faint clink of ice in a glass, her footsteps approaching through the silent house. He knew the children were asleep above him in their fanciful rooms decked out with cherubim and dinosaurs, their pastel dreams rising in the night, in the terribly still trees. And their father, in his room, slept a different kind of sleep, like other fathers up and down this street, exhausted and utterly finished with the world till next light, while his wife beside him opened her eyes, suddenly worried about something she might have overlooked, something forgotten that flitted across her consciousness like a bat, then vanished, and she sighed and rolled over, closed her eyes again ....

The door opened and Louise stepped out and placed a short, thick tumbler in Omar's hand. He felt the coolness of the ice coming through the glass; the liquor was a pale liquid gold in the candlelight as he brought it to his mouth.

"You drink bourbon, don't you?"

"From time to time," he said. "From time to time."

"That's good bourbon."

"I can tell."

He took another swallow and stared out at the dark street.

"I love these nights," Louise said. "These hot summer nights there's nothing like a nightcap."

Omar nodded and thought, I love that word. *Nightcap.*

"Well," he said, "I was just walking. I'm not even sure what time it is."

"It must be around midnight. Not quite."

He glanced at her and thought she was probably an evening's length of drink ahead of him. He considered the comical phrases he might use to describe her condition: hammered, or knackered, or bombed. But none of these seemed an accurate definition of the deep and dreamy wooziness she was sunk in, and as she talked – about journalism and books, her days in radio and television – he admitted to himself the attraction of that condition, the inevitability, even, for any sentient adult. What was it but the dreaminess of a lush life never attained, the dream of perfect summer that sustains us through winter, the summer that's almost here, that we can taste and almost touch, but never quite arrives? The season that never really comes. And he felt amazed to realize that even at sixty or seventy some people still wait on that summer, reach for it unconsciously, fumble for it from the deep grip of their regret or bitterness, and not even bitterness of the past but because they still hunger for experience, still hunger for the glamours and satisfactions of summer. Omar thought that here in the middle of his life he hadn't much knowledge of those satisfactions: their procurement too often meant the derailment of wonder. He thought Louise might be ashamed of him if he told her how many times he'd been tipsy or had sex in the past twelve months. "Good God, man! How can you live?" she'd demand, drunkenly but earnestly, and he'd be at a loss to provide an answer. Though there must be one. He was almost certain there was a reason for living like this.

She was asking him a question. He met her eye and said, "What was that?"

"I asked where you got that name. Omar. Is there a story behind it?"

The way she peered over her reading glasses at him, with her eyes slitted behind cigarette smoke, her legs in baggy shorts jauntily crossed, made him laugh and swirl the liquor in his glass.

"There is," he said. "There's a story, or half of one. My grandfather on my mother's side was a missionary in Egypt. His right hand man over there was a convert named Omar. When my grandfather preached, Omar stood beside him and translated, so there were always two preachers going at once in two different languages. Anyhow, this Omar went on to become a great Egyptian evangelist, and I'm named after him."

"An Egyptian evangelist?" Louise said, incredulity on her face. "How very odd. And have you ever been there?"

"To Egypt?" He laughed again and swallowed some bourbon and wondered if he'd ever go anywhere again, if he'd ever see another country or even get out of the city before summer ended. "No," he said, "but I have some photographs of my grandfather taken there. Or, I used to have some." And for a minute he recollected a picture of his ancestor, tall and angular, standing with another man in front of an early Cadillac with chrome fenders and white-walled tires. Both men wore fezzes and heavy black suits.

Between them, in the distance, a pyramid was visible. As a kid, Omar had gawked at the car, which the second man had shipped from America. Later, he'd been impressed that both men wore black suits under the fierce desert sun, which showed as a brown glare in the old photograph. The pyramid, on the other hand, hadn't really intrigued him. Its presence in the picture was ornamental, like the pyramid on an American dollar bill.

Louise asked another question.

"Pardon me?"

"Do you have any Scottish blood?"

He beamed at her. He was drunker than he thought.

"Oh sure," he said. "On my father's side."

"What was the name?" Louise asked. She sipped her drink. "What was the family name?"

"My father's mother was a MacLeish. I think that was it."

Louise blew smoke into the darkness beyond the candlelight.

"That was *my* name," she said. "My family is MacLeish."

She spoke as if he'd just confirmed something she'd long suspected.

"That's interesting," Omar said.

Then she asked him about himself, where he'd lived as a child, who his parents had been, what they'd done. He tried to answer accurately, but the topic seemed far away, farther than Egypt. His family seemed not to be his own but some other family he'd known indirectly or read about in books. As he spoke, he felt a thrill of loss at how far he'd drifted from his original self and contexts. He wondered what had become of the photograph with the pyramid in it, wondered if it had vanished forever with the rest of his past and why only now, in drunken reverie, he needed to see the pyramid again. Louise was telling him about growing up in Nova Scotia, but suddenly Omar saw a hot midsummer's day when he was fifteen, sixteen, visiting a cousin in a small city in upstate New York; saw himself leaving his cousin's house in an older clapboard neighbourhood and walking briefly under a hot, mottled sky that prefigured afternoon thunderstorms. He remembered the silence under the city trees and the small lawns that were just starting to brown. As he passed a nearby house, typically squat and drab – one shade of grey darker than the sky – he heard music from an open window on the ground floor. He stood and listened. It was like nothing he'd heard before. Jazz, but he didn't know jazz then and what he heard struck him as pure and wonderful, nearly frightening, as if he were listening to the aural distillation of that very moment, the magic that hid in the shifting sky and the even brown light, in the green-heavy trees and blunt American houses simmering quietly and forever in the clarity of dreams. He cocked his head and surprised himself by walking to the door of the house and pressing the buzzer. He waited, then knocked, but nobody came. Only the music moving over the heaved and fissured blacktop driveway.

Omar wondered why he thought of all that now, why he associated the mysterious music with the photograph, with a stranger who had indirectly given him his name.

"My husband loved fireworks," Louise said. "He always carted the kids great distances to see a fireworks display. God knows he had faults, but he shared what he loved with the kids."

A stab of deep, seemingly random love for the lost strangers who had been his family went through Omar, love for the lost days that had once held all the reality he could know or imagine. Now those days were extinct and he stood alone in his life. The people and houses he'd known, the familiar seasons, had disappeared. Yes, even the weather had changed. But he still had the music. The music he loved now had existed when he was a boy, though he had not known the music then. And the music he'd heard that day near his cousin's house, it too still existed, and though he couldn't name it he probably had it at home in one of his collections. It was music he knew well, perhaps Herbie Hancock's "Maiden Voyage" or something by Miles Davis. Perhaps even Coltrane playing, say, "Wise One." It still existed and bore relation to that summer day and the diminutive pyramid in the background. The truth of this struck him as vastly mysterious, important, the key to everything.

"Carrie's father taught her a lot, I can tell you. He really did."

It occurred to Omar, then, that Carrie must be sleeping in her room below them, or perhaps she had wakened at the sound of their talk and lay there hating him for once again disturbing her rest with his overloud voice, the voice that carried through earth and concrete. Hadn't she said, "You don't know the power of your own voice – "?

If she was there, in her basement room, she'd be grinding her teeth in hatred, really hating him for talking on her porch, for wandering into the meaning of her life with his musical obsessions and mystifying speech. It mystified her because he'd failed all the tests; she simply couldn't reconcile him to the reality she lived by, and Omar could scarcely bring himself to imagine that reality. Yet, he couldn't escape the conclusion that he was someone important in her life, and she in his.

"You might consider radio work," Louise offered. "I don't know what will happen with this book of yours, but radio work might be an option."

He wondered if Carrie was down there, unable to sleep, hating him.

"I used to know a lot of people at the CBC. Even five years ago I could have helped you. But I'm afraid my connections have all moved on."

Well, let her hate him. She was right to hate him. What right had he to invade her secret spaces, her sacred retreats? He hadn't meant to do it.

"Anyhow," Louise said, "it's nice that Carrie can know you. I think you might be good for her."

Omar felt as if he were rising in the dark to the treetops with the collective dreams of the household, with the simple conceptions of birthday cakes and candles and party favours, and with complicated yearnings that showed only as colours and cross-hatching. He felt like Sam the cat with wings, chasing the vague stirrings and flutterings in the great dark boughs that covered the street and connected one house to the other in endless synchronicities.

Louise stood to refill his glass.

He blinked and started up.

"I should go," he said, setting the glass near his feet.

"Have one more."

"One more," he said, repeating the chorus of the evening. "No, it's late. I should go."

His shoes made a light scuffing on the steps. He went down to the sidewalk and turned to wave. Carrie's mother lifted her hand that held a freshly lit cigarette and a glass, her face partially illumined in the wavering candlelight.

φ

The last section went on and on as Omar tried to define the ascending arc of Coltrane's life and music. Omar found his concern returning to the particular dignity of Coltrane's vision. He strained to convey the fact of this dignity, to suggest the spiritual ascent that began with technical innovation, then rediscovered the sad-sweet poignancy of the ballads and duets with Johnny Hartman, and finally fused technique and lyricism in *A Love Supreme*. From moment to moment Omar held his theme in mind, but to press it into language, into human discourse, required a clarity of insight he found difficult to sustain.

His nights alternated between hovering, ephemeral naps in which his conscious mind refused to relinquish its grip, and free falls into the bottomless depths, hypnotic and frightening, in which his soul took leave of his body. In these sleeps, he was given the knowledge of death; he knew the dissolution and recrudescence of his soul in the endless dark, becoming one with it, moving through it forever. Looking up from his sleep he beheld the dark angel that brooded above him like a parent, and into his

sleep the angel spoke, "Because you have listened as I have listened, because you have loved as I have loved, you shall be with
me forever, where I am and where love is forever...." And as he
continued to gaze upwards he saw Coltrane walking up and down
upon the vault of heaven and filling the universe with notes, filling
it with new worlds dangerous and miracle-prone as the human
soul but always pointing beyond the merely human to a higher
mode and a final reckoning towards which human destiny ran.

Omar stared into the dark where the music had been, unable to
say whether this was waking or sleep, until finally, frustrated and
alarmed in his confusion, he began to weep. And when he awoke
dry-eyed in his bed, staring into identical darkness, he began to
weep truly; this time tears of relief for being alive and for knowing
where he was, for not being stranded between two shores.

He worked on, composing and discarding, pushing his language toward the dimension of music, struggling to maintain
clarity and meaning. The mode he strove to delineate in prose,
the mode he sought to know in his life, was compounded of faith
and fate and fatalism. Faith, in Omar's thesis, was the bedrock of
the artist's rarefied dignity. Everything about Coltrane – his music,
his countenance, the grace of his hands – bespoke that dignity and
the essential seriousness of his enterprise. He had used art to
save his soul – no other way to put it – and then used it again to
tell the story of that process. His dignity traced back to his faith
in – what? In love, of course. And what was that?

Omar broke his pencil point and smacked his forehead. No,
no, what he wanted to say – By listening to the music he had
learned things. Had someone written these things or spoken
them to him, he might have missed their meaning. But by holding onto his faith, by listening to the music through the prism of
his wonder, he had learned something. Now he was trying to say
this thing, to write it. It was the thing he had wanted to tell Carrie
and even Lisa, the winsomely desperate actress working in the
bar. Fate and faith and fatalism were mixed up with love; you had

to sort love out of the mix and faith itself was the tool you sorted with. But again he faltered, for again he recalled the fragility of his wonder, the seeming inviolability of his solitude when he considered the way of the world, what people were taught to want and what they believed they truly needed to survive.

At that moment, for the first time this season, the Mister Nice Cream truck passed beneath his window trailing its calliope tune of inanity, the idiot trill of summer he'd heard a hundred times last year before the cold had banished it. He stood up and gazed after this circus-wagon apparition from childhood as if it had rolled out of the neighbourhood where he'd grown up and into this most recent of streets to play its jingle of perpetuity into his dreams, just as now, in a moment, it would pass Carrie's house, and perhaps she was just rising from her basement room after a night of drinking and racy laughter with actor cronies or some man, passing her house right now as she sat on her porch in a blue robe, a mug of hot, strong tea clasped in her hands. His mind's eye stared at her fingers wrapped around the cup as the slow, square-bodied vehicle dingled by, and he realized that none of the words in his head defined the connection between him and her – no fate, no faith, no practical affection – only the loopy tune of the fading truck, that little musical phrase they both heard in the clear, warming air right now, *now*, this instant... and he saw her face clouded in the dream of her days, the ever-lengthening history of friends and lovers, hopes and schemes on the banal-but-perennial melody of ice-cream trucks sailing through summer, another summer in their passing lives.

φ

One afternoon, feeling choked by the heat and the insufficiency of human syntax, he fell on the old sofa in the front room and half dozed, recollecting Carrie's comments about its discomforts. Hard to imagine she'd actually sat here, not so long ago. Surely he'd dreamed that episode... He closed his eyes and felt the weight of his words slide away like sand mounds washing out in the tide. He saw masses of words succumbing to the waves, lifted by the water and carried beyond consciousness, and he felt relief. He felt the sun on his face, swam out into it, walked lightly and expectantly down his street and saw that the world began at the end of it, where it met College in a cloud of golden sunshine that held the open patio of the Italian restaurant on one corner, and on the other the green produce and red flowers set around the Korean grocery. He passed between them and noted the sweet smells of the flowers, the laughter and lit cigarettes and flash of wineglasses in the sun.

Perfect afternoon in a perfect summer, he thought, and for once he was in the moment, inside the perfection of it. He strolled to his favourite pizza parlour and sat in the front that opened to the side-walk and the city air and sunlight. "Kind of Blue" came through speakers behind the counter. He sat back in the shadow and watched the cars and streetcars moving both ways on College Street, and he knew he was dreaming an absolutely real day in the world's real life, and he was wholly alive in it. Then, among the pedestrians on the other side, he picked out Carrie walking along, pausing at the display window of a shoe store. He knew her, even though she wore sunglasses and a rose-coloured brimmed hat and a light summer jacket. She looked like the young Joan Crawford, severe but glamorous. He had not remembered a shoe store being there, but he could make out the display shoes that her eyes rested on, the faintest roseate glow of them to match her hat, and he understood that he was watching Carrie in the eternal sunshine of some endless July as she stood before the shop window. And like that, comprehending his and her juxtaposition in the eternal afternoon, he knew the fact of his love for the world, he saw the bright gods swimming in the air, flashing for an instant, then again in the rippling windows of the passing streetcar. He saw Carrie as she began to walk, moving obliviously but vividly through their moment, strolling out of sight in the perfection of their day.

He stood and stepped into the heat of the sidewalk; he peered in the direction she'd been walking, but her image had vanished. For a moment longer the endless world, the eternal street, hummed and vibrated around him, and he knew he'd mistaken his grace; he'd tilted the dream by trying to keep her in it. And then the street faded, the sunshine dimmed, all went to silence, and he floated dreamlessly out of that space.

In the evenings, Omar found himself sitting in bars. He could not defuse the tension of his workday simply by stopping or averting his inward gaze; when he put the pen down or turned away from his typewriter his mind raced on to the next sentence. The only respite was to quit his apartment, hit the cooling but still active streets, and plant himself at some bar where the first drink struck like an ice chunk dropped on a hot plate.

He held the chilled glass to his forehead and closed his eyes, trying to distinguish this night from the previous one, this bar from all the others. Well, of course, he was back in Corrado's, where he'd last met Megan in the winter. The white marble and the mirrors seemed to glow with the same mellow early evening light as filled the street beyond the wide glass front of the place, light that was like a pleasant sigh at the day's close. Sitting over his cold beer, Omar thought calmly about his book. With each passing day it became clearer to him that the project had surpassed, or fallen short of, true journalism or informative non-fiction. He understood that he had wanted to make a new kind of book, not history or biography or musicology, but a type of living beatitude, an extended meditation on the sublime link between one man and his perceived world; how music mediated the world and how someone might use music to keep him connected to the world when all the usual relations had been negated or denied.

Omar looked up from his drink and scanned the premises, half-afraid he'd see Megan. Cool sweet music sprayed down from overhead while slender men and women in summer clothes came and went behind him. All day he'd reread interviews with musicians who had worked with Coltrane; he had even tracked a few down on the telephone, and what they'd told him, time and again, was that John Coltrane's greatness had lain in his extraordinary musicianship; that he had sidestepped all the old saxophone clichés, the twinkles and trills of cocktail orchestras, the fat mellowness of self-conscious solos, the bogus sex growls and the underworld signifying that were the stock-in-trade of his inferiors. But in the same breath his contemporaries invariably implied that what made Coltrane timeless, what made his music go on and on, was something in his tone and phrasings that transcended both native talent and acquired ability. It was this slippery extra-musical element that Omar felt compelled to define, that now pushed his writing to the limit of rational discourse.

He pressed the cool glass to his forehead again and scrolled back the argument of his text, reviewing it in his mind's eye like a Möbius strip that kept rerunning the delicate logic and actual prose of his book, inserting better words in particular sentences while holding his central thesis to one side. His working theory that the late-middle period of ballads and meditations had been essential to the album *A Love Supreme* and later breakthroughs struck him as solid enough, but had he demonstrated sufficiently Coltrane's deliberate postponement of further innovations in order to pursue the transcendent lyricism of the ballads? The external evidence was circumstantial: Coltrane himself, knowing the futility of trying to describe a vision, offhandedly attributed the lyrical detour to a technical problem with his instrument's mouthpiece. Most critics chalked it up to commercial pressure to produce sales after the mixed reactions to his Village Vanguard dates.

Omar felt a twinge of that woozy, groping feeling of being on thin ice. Where did he get off using terms like "beatitude" and "transcendent"? Was he, a man who could only play the typewriter, a fool for trying to render in accessible English what Coltrane himself had cannily avoided discussing? Somehow he must convey that the lyrical period was not merely an interlude, a respite from creative fury, but an absolute necessity for what came later. In standards such as "Lush Life" and "What's New?" Coltrane seemed to be weighing the sweetness and briefness of his days against a vision of the Eternal, the heightened losses of mortal time against the unending wonder that superseded time.

Inwardly, almost audibly, Omar groaned. How could he use such language? How could he say such things in a book his publisher hoped to sell?

He glanced toward the entrance and realized he was gazing directly into the eyes of a man sitting down a few stools, near the Plexiglas front.

The man grinned and lifted his chin.

"What's this music? Where do I know it from?" He spoke in a clear, personal voice that matched the light in his eye. "I know I know this from somewhere."

Omar tilted his head and listened. Someone was playing "Deep Purple" on a theramin.

Omar told the man and the man shook his head and lit a cigarette. Still grinning, he blew the smoke upward and squinted one eye.

"An instrument that always gave me the creeps," the man said.

He drew on his cigarette, exhaled and asked Omar if he could join him. Omar looked at the man's loosened tie and pale short-sleeved shirt. A lonely salesman, perhaps, or an aging computer geek just off work.

The man blew one last billow of smoke, stubbed out his cigarette, and brought his drink around the bar and sat down beside Omar.

The man put out his hand and said, "Ron Dittmar."

Omar shook his hand, "Omar Snow."

"Omar! Now there's a name you don't hear everyday. How'd you get a name like that? You don't look like an Omar."

"I know."

"Sounds like the name of a terrorist or a famous running back."

"Yes, it's wasted on me."

"Used to be a Sixties group that featured the theramin," the man said.

Omar thought for a moment.

"Lothar and the Hand People. They had one."

Ron Dittmar looked at Omar.

"You sound like some kind of expert. Are you in the business?"

"The business? No — "

The other man called out for a refill of gin and tonic.

"I only drink it in the summer. Sorry, you were saying."

"Sometimes I write about music."

"No kidding? Like what? Books?"

"Lots of stuff. Yeah, a few books."

"You working on one now?"

Omar glanced at the other man and shrugged.

"Yeah? You're working on one now? What's it about?"

Omar swallowed some beer. The music had changed to the popular Count Basie version of "April in Paris." As a kid Omar had listened to the Count's resonant voice at the finish, calmly ordering his men to play it, "One more time." And then, the whole band coming down hard on those last lush riffs and the Count coming back again with, "One more once!" and the band pouring it on. Omar had loved it.

"It's about John Coltrane. The part I'm working on now is."

"Coltrane? God, I used to live with a woman who was insane about Coltrane. She played *A Love Supreme* for days on end, until I begged her to turn it off. Thought I'd lose my mind."

"A lot of people have that reaction to it," Omar said.

"I don't mean to say I didn't like the record," Ron Dittmar said. "*A Love Supreme* was one of those seminal Sixties albums. Everybody remembers hearing it for the first time, where they were and all that. It's just not the sort of thing I'd put on after a hard day's work."

Looking sideways, Omar noted Ron Dittmar's thin blond hair and tired face, the blue-capped pen in his shirt pocket. Dittmar wore a wedding ring and smelled faintly of perspiration and aftershave. Omar wondered if he might be a kind of messenger or sign, like the giant mollusk-saxophone atop the artists' co-op down the street.

"I was crazy nuts over this woman," Dittmar said. "And she was just crazy. Beautiful, but crazy, this Jewish woman who ended up being some kind of Voodoo priestess in New Orleans. Oh man, what a time. We were living in a converted barn loft out in the Eastern Townships the summer she kept playing the record. It was already six or seven years old, I believe."

Ron Dittmar took off his glasses and peered into his drink.

"We had a major rat infestation that was totally out of control. We were overrun and had just about decided to move out of this otherwise perfect loft space when my girlfriend got this idea. One night at full moon she put A Love Supreme on the stereo and cranked it to the max, and I'm telling you – these big old speakers that come up to your waist, no one around for miles – we just let it rip. Like a physical force going through the foundation. What a night. It was summer and all the windows and doors were open. The rafters quaked. The whole countryside felt it. We finished a bottle of Captain Morgan and played it until dawn."

Omar waited for what came next.

"Next day, no more rats. You could hear them clearing out all night. You could hear them running off in the dark."

Omar finished his beer and pushed the empty glass away. He met Ron Dittmar's eyes in the long mirror behind the bar.

"A good story," Omar said, "I can use that one."

Dittmar blinked and straightened. "What?" he said. "You don't believe me? Here, let me buy you one."

Omar thanked him automatically and asked him what he did for a living.

"I work for Bombardier." He smiled at Omar. "I repossess private jets."

Omar nodded dully, as if he might have guessed.

"Tricky business, but I'm just another repo man when you get down to it." He tapped Omar's shoulder. "Well, I better run. Good luck writing about music."

He slapped some bills on the marble counter, waved at the bartender, and walked out into the urban twilight. Omar sat over the pint Ron Dittmar had bought him and watched the summer couples strolling by and crossing the street. The music misted around him, pleasant and fresh as a casual blessing: down the bar a woman laughed deliciously, and suddenly Omar knew that whatever became of his book, whether he published it or not, whether or not he retrieved a dime for the months of obsessive work, he had entered at last a plane he had always believed in and wanted and wondered about. Finally he'd arrived at that rarefied place where he was both particle and wave, both inside and outside the moment the way music could be both inside and outside time, the way it sublimely infused and flowed around those dimensions, the way he had been both inside Ron Dittmar's story as the man relived it in imagination and outside as he sat here, his eyes wandering over the bottles and bodies and changing light while certain sentences from his book appeared and rearranged themselves and chased new ones. Whatever became of his words on the actual page, he had learned this, he had become a sort of music now and again in the long contemplation and hard exercise of the senses that his book had demanded. The knowledge of this – of what he had briefly become – was a sort of ecstasy. He felt it flowing around him, in the sounds and movements of the night. He held it for as long as he could. Then he paid his bill and stepped outside.

The way his shoes met the sidewalk delighted him; he took a voluptuary thrill from his footsteps on the planet. He held the warm, electric air in his lungs.

Well, he'd had a few drinks. No point mystifying that.

Yet something else was still in him, and he was in it. He had placed himself in the flow of living waters and there was no telling where they would take him now.

As he crossed the intersection a splash of silver turned his head: cameras and kliegs and cables lined the street; a long white truck on the sidewalk. Omar waited on the far curb. Serious-looking men and athletic young women milled importantly on the street and busied themselves with dollies, tripods, cellphones. They wore ball caps and cut-off jeans and bright running shoes. They were engaged, Omar knew, in the urgent business of the world. He watched a tall, stooped man with shaggy silver hair study his clipboard and speak into his phone like a company commander staging an attack. In the future, Omar mused, fame as a commodity will cease to exist. The fame in the world will be all used up. Our human capacity to believe in it, to react to it, will be expended and ultimately negated by all the fifteen-minute wonders, the myriad faces thrown into the spotlight and then washed under by the new myriad. By God, Omar thought, I have a glamour in my heart you can never fill your screens with ... you'll never know the slippery stuff my soul is made of....

He smiled and looked over his shoulder as if his thoughts were audible; he folded his arms and felt inexplicably proud and graceful and cool and strong. He felt his figure shining in the eventide, shining against the bath of white-blue and silver light a hundred yards down the street.

More activity: bodies bunched and separated, and the star of the scene or commercial or whatever it was struck a pose beside a sleek little car; the big lights poured down on him like silver rain; a silence fell; then Omar recognized Harris in a handsome suit leaning against the car. Whether he was selling the suit or the car, Omar couldn't say, but it was definitely Harris – who did not own a car and perhaps not even a suit; who came to acting late and indirectly when he was stone broke and someone suggested he give it a try; who took these gigs so he could travel to Paris or sit in his tiny apartment and translate obscure European poets. Harris, who never had a significant other the whole time Omar had known him, who went out maybe once a month and even then, usually, at the behest of a woman, who mistakenly equated his looks with a character she knew from experience. But the lady had erred. Good old Harris. Poor old Harris. Poor old everyone....

As he watched his friend work, Omar told himself the show was just the show, the world just the world, and humans were still human. He thought of Carrie, brooding in her mother's basement, waiting for the princely ideal to rescue her from a fate beneath her beauty and intelligence. If only he could tell her! If only he could mate the glamour of his soul to the shine of her flesh, make new the old mystery of the ripe world accepting the silver flash – the Sons of God meeting the Daughters of Men – what glorious moments they might make of the summer!

Something beeped, and down the street four or five people clustered around Harris. He was working down there. Making an honest buck. Omar blinked and shook himself awake. For a minute there he'd felt the cameras trained on him, catching the glamour that came off his soul like the nimbus of his eternal body, the light that outshone all the movies. That shining light, he decided, is what Coltrane played. Nothing less than the shine on the human soul transmuted into sound.

Well, it was probably the drink, but he felt interested and alive. Darkness fell softly, thickly, and he happily plunged into it, turning toward his street. A nearly full moon blazed down and his fluid shadow preceded him as he ambled, chanting the street names – Clinton, Grace, Beatrice – like zany poetry or a mantra only he could pronounce.

He walked on the east side of his street, behind the row of cars that stretched the length of it, until his eye fell on Carrie's house on the other side. The first-floor window was lit with soft lamps that showed the dignified mantelpiece and the sea-green wall around it. He went on a few paces and looked over his shoulder. The angle now revealed Carrie on the sofa, under the lamp, reading a magazine. She wore cream-coloured pyjamas and her hair fell over her glasses. Omar stopped and watched her turn a page, touch her glasses, a warm moony glow on her face beneath her dark red hair. He saw her as a teenager reading a novel, absorbing scenes dreamily, blankly even, a rare calm at the end of her hectic social day. But mostly it was the soft green light and the room's comfort that drew his imagination; it was the glow of human ease, set in the perfect sweetness of evening that blossomed for him at his observation post in the dark. He heard the final robin trill regretfully behind him; the night-laden trees seemed to nod over the houses and parked cars; the very pavement of the street returned the day's warmth into the darkness that he breathed and he felt so close to the literal image of his hope that he could almost touch it. He steadied himself against a warm fender – then started when he felt a pressure on his ankle: Sam the cat slipped between his feet, mewling in cranky and highly articulate Abyssinian, and Omar, unconsciously mimicking Carrie, said, "Sam boy!" and reached down to rub his neck. The cat pressed a sinewy haunch against Omar's shin, purred and complained and vanished under the car. Omar straightened, looked across the street to where Carrie sat reading. At that moment her eyes came up and blinked behind her glasses as though she'd heard Sam or sensed the tipsy man in the shadows. Her eyes seemed too peer into his, then dropped to her book again, and Omar, taking one last glance, moved on toward his house.

Suddenly he recollected that Harris had accused him of deflecting Carrie with irony. Could that possibly be true? He, Omar, believed he had less irony in him than anyone he knew. Any music writer, anyhow....

As he walked, he stared at the grinning moon and blue-glowing sky over the rooftops and streets and alleys that honeycombed the night, and he woozily puzzled over the way Harris and Carrie and everyone else hurried through the maze of it, pushing with or against the current, now and again drifting into contact, knowing each other just now in this place, this moment, that would never come again. Knowing each other, also, in fate and faith, at peculiar distances that transcended time, that lasted forever. Once more he admitted these relations were all in his head; one more time he swore they were utterly real, that they were, in fact, a kind of love. Perhaps the only kind that lasted. The music had taught him this. He couldn't say how, other than that in the long contemplation of its essences, its use of silence as well as sound, a certain light had accrued. But the music had taken him to the threshold, and with an agony that was nearly delicious in its completeness, he again despaired of putting this light into words.

Toward dawn he dreamed of a red dust storm that buffeted the earth like a final scourge and cleansing, and he thought he saw the silver saxophone-cephalopod riding the wild wind above the planet. Through red dust gales he saw that the silver nautilus, which seemed to blow the world apart, was really starting everything over again. He could almost see the unformed notes that would bloom into starfish and strange flowers, into hummingbirds and giraffes and waterwheels and martini glasses. Those primal notes were about to burst free of the horn's curiously squared yet shell-like bell when the wind rose to a pitched wail – a door banged open –

Omar sat up in bed, his heart pounding, and stared through the wide-open door to the dull pink glow on his outer deck. The whirlwind flew about his room and knocked something over on the dresser. He held his breath and peered at the orange-pink radiance outside.

And then the wind subsided, the light lost its hue, and it was merely morning – just another morning in the world, with a few sparrows twittering in the near distance.

φ

For three days he couldn't write. He reread what he had written of his final chapter, riding the surge and peak of its wave, stopping abruptly where the wave flowed outward into light and, he feared, beyond comprehension. He thought there must be a name for that final stretch of the wave. Surfers or physicists must have a name. But the answer, he knew, lay in the music, always the music, and he sat and listened for hours, working hard, processing everything he heard. On an impulse, he pulled out an old Monk LP from 1957 – that pivotal year – and listened carefully. It featured an unlikely septet that included Coleman Hawkins and Art Blakey and Coltrane. They were slightly inept with Monk's music, but the very idea of Coltrane and Hawkins together behind Monk excited him. He kept playing the first five minutes of the record: it began with just the horns playing the nineteenth-century hymn, "Abide With Me," then went almost directly into "Well, You Needn't." Omar loved the hymn, a motto of courage and spirituality at the start, then the pure swing of Monk's tune rolling out of it. He loved the moment, two minutes into the song, where Monk finished his solo and called out, "Coltrane! Coltrane!" and the tenor swooped in like a splendid bull entering the ring. And Coltrane's name wasn't even mentioned on the album cover! An imperfect recording, to be sure, but full of history and portents and intricate secrets.

On the third day, after an entire morning of hard listening – listening with his body and brain and spirit – Omar staggered out into the sunlight and automatically drifted down to the Starbuck's on College Street, where he sat staring at his cup and waited for his mind to unclench. A new jazz loop played today. He stared at the steam rising over his coffee and let the notes lightly pelt his brain like a summer shower. At a nearby table a poised, long-faced Englishwoman sat with a squat, pale man in a black jogging suit, their voices raised in earnest discussion about a film they were working on. Plainly, they were partners in the enterprise. Co-producers, probably. The Englishwoman spoke in world-weary tones, with her lean, brown arms crossed on the table. To Omar, her gaunt muscle definition suggested an emotional intensity that required physical obsession to keep it in balance. A cellphone chirped and she reached into her canvas sack. She spoke tersely into the little black instrument.

"I don't care what Laszlo says. I need an answer. Today."

She gripped the phone lightly while her eyes searched the ceiling. Omar studied her enamelled nails against the phone's glossy chrome.

"Just do it today," she said. "You know the score here."

She touched the phone and dropped it into her bag and faced her companion.

"That was Teddy in L.A.," she said. "They're looking at it."

"Now we wait," said the pale man primly.

They stood and walked out of the café onto the sunny street, where they embraced perfunctorily and went their separate ways.

Again Omar wondered how long this street had been here, and then how long this coffee shop had been on it – two years, tops. And how long people had been making deals like this, over the phone and on the fly, and how long the city itself had been a kind of shadow Hollywood? This town, when it was poor and puritanical, had once been an authentic place. Now it was only a concept, like a vast shopping mall. Perhaps his street was real, the street he shared with Carrie and her family, but the rest was meaningless energy in the illusion mall. Its citizens were TV anchors or data analysts or personal trainers. They shaped white noise and managed images. And yet, the haze of nervous excitement that gripped the city interested him; in some ancillary fashion he was part of it. His dreaminess was tolerated. The old industrial world would have persecuted him, while this one simply abandoned him to his solitude. But the old world had succumbed to the movies and now people went to films the way their grandparents had gone to church.

The music, Omar posited, was Step One on the long road back to church.

He reached for his cup and saw that his hand shook. This thinking was not without palpable effects on the flesh. And the book, it never ended, it would never end, it would take him over the edge. He tried to consider it objectively. Was he afraid of finishing it? Maybe he believed his grace would end when the book was finished. But he was closing in on something, he sensed the imminence of revelation that would come with the completion of his book. When the work was done, he'd have no will to fight those sleeps that were like slow descents through endless underwater caverns. But something else would be given, some knowledge or earthly comfort that might redeem all the strain and deprivation.

With a start he realized he was hearing Coltrane; it took him a moment to ascertain that indeed "Naima" played on the new loop, and he thought of Carrie and knew for certain now she was someone important in his life.

At that instant, in the music, his sense of their connection struck like a physical shock, an ecstatic logic that tied together everything he'd been thinking for months, and he not only saw the saxophone notes in the dull commercial air, but each one opened like a bruise, like a purple flower that held his meaning, his destiny, right there in the slanting afternoon sunshine, and before he could think again someone held a tray of tiny paper cups toward him and obediently he took one and the notes bloomed around him and he understood why he was here. For this was the church of John Coltrane, and he beheld the musician in a threadbare checked vest and bow tie, the small platter of cups balanced perfectly on the yellow broad tips of his fingers, so long and elegantly jointed, like sculpture, and Coltrane said, "Drink this in remembrance of love – " and Omar looked into the paper cup and recognized the enormous solitude of his heart and drank it down through a little green plastic straw that made a gurgling noise at the end.

Someone across the room asked, "What is this exactly?" And the girl serving the samples answered, "Lemon-mango frappuccino," and Omar hid his eyes behind his hand.

He felt like himself again only after the music stopped, only after Coltrane completed his meandering reverie of acceptance and loss and love for the exquisite patina on the world's everyday surface, the numinous finish on its common objects and the holy spirit in everything.

φ

He worked more calmly now, though what seemed to be sensible workmanlike habits were more like daily walks on water. He wrote and wrote without looking down. But the end hovered in the near distance. Omar knew it was coming. One day, he knew, he'd finish a sentence and that would be that.

June waned into heat and long evenings and the unfolding promise of endless summer. Late one afternoon Omar left his desk to step out for some milk. On the street, looking around, he realized today was Saturday, another weekend, and already people were flee-ing the city for cottages or making dinner dates, any of a dozen bright excursions to celebrate full summer. A certain excitement thrummed the air, a spirit of anticipation that even he, from his remove of abstraction, perceived in the movements of pedestrians, in their expectant voices and faces. He thought of Carrie and Megan and others he hadn't seen in weeks; he knew they'd be out there, swimming in the summer gaiety, not only absorbing the loveliness of the evening but adding to it, becoming it, losing their bad dreams in the night's general glamour because their glamour matched it, complimented it, put firm shape and flesh on the excitement every-one saw and felt.

He bought his carton of milk and drifted back to work, back to his desk, pausing now and then to remind himself that he still dwelled in grace, that whatever happened or didn't happen was still inevitable and proper, so long as he observed his disciplines and stayed true to the music. On the other hand, he still felt vague trepidation about reaching the book's end. He feared it might deliver him to an even deeper and more final solitude, a place of ironclad silence that went on forever.

Soon after dark, putting in one last hour of work, Omar heard a dull thump and the old window glass rattled lightly in the wooden frames. He raised his head. Another thump, like an explosion in the distance. He went to the back bedroom, opened the door to his small deck, and stepped into a new and thrilling darkness. Something was going on out there. The air shuddered and the southern sky opened into blue and red lights that blossomed and drifted over the distant and invisible harbour. Omar stared while the fireworks rose and spread across the blue night sky like crazy neon snakes, like apocalyptic scribbling, and he thought he heard the collective gasps and sighs of the entire city in attendance. One after another the rockets rose, weaving wonky coloured tails across the shining blue, each burst and explosion more extravagant than the last. The sky filled with magnificent umbrellas opening into silver and gold. Starry wheels revolved fatefully over the rooftops. Then a pause; the sky emptied; fiery bits of amber and orange dribbled down. Omar stood and stared; he held himself taut, waiting for what came next.

A solitary red rocket shot lazily up and up and peaked with a distinct pop that formed a pulsing red star above the city's limit. A chambered red heart, plimming and shimmering and ringed by fire that hung like a blazing medallion over the expectant world, and Omar saw that it was his heart, or the heart of his Lord, the Sacred Heart of Summer that he had hungered to know. He stared while it lengthened and fell, particle by fiery particle, into the vault of darkness over the harbour. In the moment it ceased to exist, the rumbling sky flooded with many colours, myriad patterns, explosions within explosions that converged and opened toward him like the terrible hand of God, and he stepped back into his darkened bedroom because the hand was all around him and Omar knew that it could never be written or possessed in fact or flesh or sound.

He stood gaping in the closeness of his room, and then, fumbling, rushing, he changed his clothes, put on his chinos and old huarache shoes and a turquoise rayon shirt, and hurried out of the house.

The sidewalk carried families and laughing couples toward College Street; above the trees, spotlights plied the avenue of sky. Omar crossed and cut through the short alley to the next street over: he did not want to pass Carrie's house tonight. Tonight he would simply follow the crowd, follow the inevitability that swam in the evening air like a living organism. On this street too the sidewalks flowed with people moving toward the lights and sounds of College. When he reached the intersection, he realized that some kind of festival was in full swing.

Omar hovered on the brink of the crowd, human currents that streamed to his left and his right on the longer street. He breathed the living air, shivered and plunged in. He found a slower current within the brisker one and let it carry him down the street. He passed vendors hawking peanuts and balloons; sausages sizzled and pastries simmered on little grills in front of bakeries and cafés. Small espresso machines pumped aromatic steams into the evening. Omar paused, was literally turned around by the surging bodies; he stepped into the street to drink in the sound. Trios of teenage girls with long black hair and linked arms threw back their heads and laughed a kind of full-throated calliope music. Young men lit cigarettes and surveyed the scene through slitted eyes. Omar moved on, sidestepping babies in strollers and dogs on leashes. At the corner a knot of pedestrians tightened around seven musicians playing trumpets and steel drums. What joy, Omar thought, to toss those notes into the general cacophony of the crowd, like metallic threads running through a bright woven blanket. He listened a moment longer. Looking down, he saw that he was surrounded by children, darkly brooding little boys with tiny Italian flags in their chubby fists. He stepped around them and walked on.

As he made his way he thought about what he had tried to say in his book, the language wave that had washed him up on this night. The words were his bane, but the effort had clarified him. Somehow the music and writing about music had brought him here. The final product, the beatitude he had wanted to make, might fall short, but the time he'd taken to listen and tell what he'd heard had not been wasted. He moved on, thinking about what he had seen in the sky. It seemed to him to be both a reward and an omen, a blessing and a sign he must attend. He stopped, jostled by hips and elbows. He heard a girl call his name. He swore he'd heard the voice of a girl, or a child, who knew him in this unfathomable crowd. He recollected someone saying that Bix Biederbecke's cornet sounded like a girl singing hymns in a field, and it dawned on him that he knew that girl. Her voice, the very quality of it, turned the paradigm around, and in the voice that called to him he heard the cornet hymn to summer and sweetness and the moment's blossom; this moment, like the heart in the sky, had arrived as reward for his faith, his labour; it dotted his existence with a heart-shaped Epistrophy that summed up and culminated all his wonder.

Remembering what he'd seen in the sky, he felt himself teetering on the very edge of fate; he felt the music and his work and the girl's voice converging in the night. He felt the sky against his skin. The street before him pulsed with light.

He reached the curb and waited with the crowd while a small, blue three-wheeled car skittered through the intersection. Someone bumped him, just enough to make him step off the curb. He caught himself, turned, and saw Carrie, her face creased in laughter.

"Omar, I've been trailing you for half a block! Didn't you hear me?"

He stepped back onto the sidewalk, grinned, shook his head.

She laughed again, the music of it mixing with the huge din.

"Where are you going?" she asked him. "Are you headed anywhere in particular?"

"In particular? No, I guess not."

"I'm supposed to meet my friend Irma down the street. Did you see the fireworks? Mom and I watched from Duncan's deck but the trees blocked most of them."

"I saw them," Omar said. He looked at her: "Did you see the heart?"

"The what?" She laughed and knotted her brow. "We missed a lot. But what we saw were great. Come with me and we'll find Irma."

She touched his wrist and he fell in behind her as she pressed through the throng, now and then glancing back to shout something he couldn't quite hear. A white light like a living haze hung over their heads and Omar thought that years from now he'd remember this night, the people and the quality of light and darkness and the striking woman he'd known, the actress who had lived with her mother on his street. She was waiting, up ahead, with a half-amused grimace.

"Sorry," he called, and he hurried after her through the people and the white light that vibrated with music and voices, through the smells of food and coffee and perfume and cigarettes.

Two blocks down they veered into a bar full of young men and women in scant summer clothes, stylish shoes and expensive haircuts – a caste distinctly different from the families outside. The air throbbed with ambient techno-rock and theatrical laughter. He and Carrie fit themselves onto the tall stools at the curved end of the bar. Carrie asked the barman for two bottles of Italian beer and turned to Omar: "Can you get this round? I haven't worked in two weeks."

Omar paid the man and poured his beer into a small glass. Carrie clinked her bottle to his glass and asked the woman on her right for a cigarette. Omar smiled and looked around. His encounters with Carrie were so infrequent and accidental; each time he seemed to be meeting her for the first time, and he saw her too-blue eyes and the grimly perfect mouth as if he'd never seen them before.

She looked up at the bartender, an ageless man with a shaved head who had paused on the other side of the bar to sip some water from a glass. With a small, harsh laugh in her throat she called, "What are you looking at?" and the man smiled and resumed his work with a knowing air. Omar's first thought was that he, like everyone else, had simply been staring at her almost ostentatiously lovely face. But as he drank the cold beer it occurred to Omar that perhaps Carrie came here often with another man or men, and the bartender, in an impish moment, had let her know he knew.

Omar looked at her and tried to see what the bartender had seen, what the world saw as she pursued her daily business. He noted the tan sleeveless top she wore, the glow on her shoulders – and if she asked him what he was looking at, he'd have to say he didn't know. He didn't know what he was looking at.

Carrie ordered another beer and a shot of scotch.

"I wish that Irma would show up," she said, scanning the room over her shoulder.

Irma, Omar thought, was not the name of anyone he thought she might know.

Carrie bummed a second cigarette and tapped it on the counter.

"How's the book going? When did I see you last? I probably owe you a phone call."

He told her the book was almost finished, but the last bit was proving tricky. He said he couldn't recall the last time they'd met, which was nearly true, for his imaginations and glimpses of her had seemed like actual encounters with vital exchanges.

"I meet you at the funniest times," she said.

"How's that?"

"I always run into you at a point when something is happening with me, or has just happened."

She lit the cigarette and stared at the line of liquor bottles in front of them. For a minute she vanished into the enigmatic space she carried with her; her face hardened behind the smoke and he saw her plainly and humanly, saw her as peevish and pouty, but also as the specific shape of his hope.

She said, "I had another dream about you."

He waited. He asked, "What was it? What was the dream?"

"I can't remember now. Really, I can't. Don't worry, it'll come back to me. They always do."

She knocked back the scotch and took a quick hit off the cigarette.

"Where's that Irma?" she said. "She swore she'd be here by ten."

Omar ordered two more beers. The small green bottles were cold and beaded. The piped soundtrack of abstracted electronic muzak beat down on the patrons behind them. Omar watched Carrie's tapered fingers lift the bottle to her lips. For a moment he felt tempted to tell her about their fatedness, how there could be love without being in love, how there could be an ultimate relation without a relationship. Though they lived in different spaces – he on the outside of the vast and vibrating urban cell and she within it – they were fated to arrive at the same crossroads, fated to the lush life both spaces eventuated in if they refused to decide. But sitting there, in her energy and aura, he saw how she conducted her life in pure moments, moments with an intensely particular charge, but no larger meaning. Isolated moments that did not add up, except in the strictly physical process of aging and disillusionment. It was her way, he realized, to be wholly in the moment but not truly with the other people in it. Or, again, to know them only as cohabitants of that moment and not as individuals with pasts or tomorrows. It was an actor's way. And this both discouraged and excited him.

"You know what?" she said. "I don't think Irma's going to show. I think we've waited long enough. I'd like to hit the street again. What about you?"

"Yes," he said. "Let's go."

He paid for the last round and they went out, re-engaging the light and sound and surging throngs, and again he felt the inevitability that had delivered him to this moment. He felt the nearness of it in the crowds and the funky night air. As he pushed along with Carrie the pale human faces lifted with smiles as if they approved of them as a couple.

They passed a jazz combo set up on the corner, an electric piano and bass and drums, knocking out neat light-hearted riffs. The drummer smiled at Carrie. She raised a hand and they walked on. She paused before an open grill in front of a bistro.

"Oh man," she said. "Those smell good. They make great sausage sandwiches here."

"Do you want one?"

"Maybe we could share it."

Omar bought a sandwich and the vendor halved it with a small, sharp-looking knife. They stood back and ate the spicy meat and watched passers-by.

"This is good," Omar said.

"I'll need another drink soon."

Carrie pointed at a white convertible parked on the side street.

"God, it's beautiful," she said with passing awe.

Omar shifted his gaze from the car. She dropped a nub of bread into the big silver waste container.

"Let's find that drink," she said.

They drifted through the jumbled column of bodies that filed unsteadily down the sidewalk, taking everything in, glancing from side to side. Across the street a skinny white kid played "It's Now or Never" on a tenor sax. Omar paused to listen. Carrie peered at the player and waited for him.

Walking together again, she said, "Now I remember my dream. You were showing me your book, the actual printed book. The cover had angel wings and saxophones and a big red heart with a blue note in it. When you opened it the pages had musical scores instead of sentences. But it was a kind of music I'd never seen. More like cuneiform or some extinct language."

They walked slowly. Omar watched his feet and listened.

"You kept asking me to sing it," she said. "Even though you'd written it you couldn't read the notes. It was odd."

Omar waited for more. He guessed there was something else to the dream, but he was afraid to ask.

They walked until she touched his elbow and steered him into another café. Behind the bar, an older man who looked like a benign high-school teacher greeted Carrie by name. He rubbed the counter with a clean rag and asked after her mother. They sat in front of him and folded their hands.

Carrie said, "We need two beers and two shots of tequila, Vince, and some lime slices."

The man set the drinks in front of them. He came back with six or seven lime slices on a saucer. Carrie drank off half her beer and swivelled all the way around on the barstool. She propped her elbows on the counter behind her and studied the crowd.

"I like this place," she said. "I used to come here with my boyfriend in college. When we broke up he literally got down on his knees and wept. The only man who ever did that for me."

She turned back to the counter and downed the shot.

Omar doubted the bit about men not crying. He bet they made awful scenes, shouting and breaking things. He knew he'd do the same. He drank the tequila and thought that if he let himself, right now, he could cry, too. Easily. He felt his eyes grow hot and wet. He shook his head and smiled.

"Have a lime," Carrie said, pushing the saucer toward him.

He crushed the tart fruit between his teeth and sucked it.

"It's been awhile since I've done shooters," he told her.

"They work for me in summer."

In the mirror behind the bottles they watched the people push in and out of the café. Omar noticed a man wearing glasses with green frames who sat a few seats to Carrie's right. The man seemed to stare at Omar, then look away when they made eye contact in the mirror. Before long he stood and put a bill on the bar. He glided down the mirror, passed Omar and took two steps back.

"Excuse me," he said, leaning on the counter. Omar turned his head and saw the man studying him with a bright and narrowed expression.

He said, "You're an actor, aren't you? Haven't I seen you in something recently?"

"Me?" Omar said. He glanced at Carrie, then faced the man again. "Not me. *She's* an actor. You've probably seen her before." The man stared at Omar as if he didn't believe him, a sardonic small grin beneath his green spectacles.

"My mistake," he said knowingly. Then he turned and left.

Omar caught Carrie's eye in the mirror.

"That's a first," he said. She didn't smile.

"Let's finish up here and go somewhere else," she said. "I'd like to get back outside."

Omar paid for the drinks and they wandered out to the sidewalk. Carrie looked left and right as if trying to decide something. The air had cooled slightly. She started walking and Omar followed. She mentioned cigarettes and Omar ducked into a doughnut shop and bought her brand. He handed the pack to her on the sidewalk and without speaking they drifted toward the limit of the strip, where the bars and restaurants gave way to shabby offices and copy shops. Omar thought the great night over the eastward city looked black and impenetrable, as if civilization – the shining dream of it – faded away at the perimeter of their neighbourhood. They stopped beside the big Portuguese Seventh Day Adventist church and stared at its lugubrious front, brown and blunt with a massiveness like the background architecture in Renaissance paintings. A lit sign near the sidewalk read, "ASSISTA Daniel E Apocalipse Sem Misterios." They stood for a minute with the bright noise just behind them.

Carrie said, "Have you ever been with someone you thought was too good for you?"

Omar looked at her.

"Too good? What do you mean, too good?"

She stared toward the city, her face beautifully rigid.

"Tell me," he said. "I'm interested."

She glanced at him, shrugged, and turned back toward the neighbourhood. Omar watched her go, then followed. Back in the bump and clamour of the celebration, she told him about a TV job she'd landed, a slick drama set in the city's financial district. She'd play an academic turned porn star, she said, and mentioned the research she'd done for the role. In her judgment, many porn films were better than most Hollywood B-movies: they were less violent and they gave the actors, particularly women, more say in the process. All of this sounded to Omar like something she'd heard from a shabby director, or even lines she was rehearsing for the part. As he listened he realized that Lisa, the actress-bartender down the street, had auditioned for the same show.

"Those are the only parts I get anymore," Carrie said with a short laugh. "I guess I'm destined to play unhappy intellectuals or whores."

Omar wanted to say something about destiny, he wanted to show the logic behind it, and how there could be love behind the logic. At that moment the crowd parted and a young woman in a loose lavender-blue dress stepped off the curb, and in the instant of passing they beheld her elegantly long face, dark eyes, long black hair and two short, horribly withered arms: Carrie caught her breath mid-sentence and leaned into him as they crossed to the curb. Then she moved away and finished her comment, and as they walked Omar thought of the spring, the sex scene she'd described as they'd strolled the street after dinner. The film, he recalled, would be released in the autumn, and he supposed he'd never see it. No, he wouldn't have to squirm through that one. But the idea of such highly personalized pain, remote yet somehow inescapable, held another kind of certainty beyond intention or will, and again he perceived a bright inevitability flashing all around like laughter.

Carrie walked slowly, holding an unlit cigarette near her face, glancing at the faces swimming by. The night had changed: fewer families on the street, but the bars were jammed. Periodically she nodded and smiled at someone.

"Every fourth person is from the industry," she said.

"I get that feeling every day."

Omar considered how she held the cigarette. He recognized it again as an actor's gesture. It seemed possible that her character and mystery, as Harris had once suggested, were merely a series of shapely gestures strung over a constant of petulance and discontent. And yet, in their way, in their pure mode of being, the gestures were enough. He breathed deep and held the night in his chest.

"Here," she said. "Let's try this."

He followed her into a bar less crowded than the last. Loud rhythm & blues came down from the speakers in back.

They stood at the end of the counter and ordered pints. Carrie seemed unaffected by the alcohol she'd already consumed. Omar found matches, lit her cigarette, grinned.

She blew smoke and peered at him.

"What's the joke?"

"I don't know," he said happily. "I'm probably a little drunk. And the music. Not every night you hear great stuff like this."

"Who is it?"

He cocked his head and listened to the singer, a black woman with a voice like a freight train rocking through a swampy southern night. He snapped his fingers and squinted.

"I know I know it."

"She's great," Carrie said.

Omar felt the vivid grin on his face.

"Let's dance," he said.

Her eyes flickered to his; without a word, just as their beer arrived, she placed her cigarette in the ashtray and led him to an open spot on the floor. She placed his hands on her waist and shoulder, fit herself into his arms, and started to move in an improvised slow dance. Omar, startled, felt the deep physical empathy flow from her body to his. The female voice, loud and harsh, but loaded with impossible hope and physical yearning, sang out, *Candy, why I call my sugar Candy, he understands me ...* while their feet shuffled in small circles on the tile floor.

"We've never danced before," Carrie said, close to his shoulder.
"You're a good dancer."

The music, lazy and blue, pushed them from side to side.

"I'm very fluid," she said, and Omar believed her and knew
something he hadn't known before.

He spoke just above her ear: "Did you sing the music in my
book?"

She arched her neck and looked at him. "The music in what?"

"The book in your dream. My book."

She moved close again and he thought he could feel her
thinking. "I don't know," she said. "Maybe. Maybe I did."

The song finished. Another began. She laughed and started
toward the bar. They stood in front of their full glasses.

"You're a lousy dancer," she said as she lifted her glass.

He smiled. "I know."

The bartender, a bright-faced blonde in a man's white shirt,
overheard them as she passed and said, "But that was just what we
needed here. Some dancing. You two made my night."

Omar asked her about the music.

"That's Big Maybelle. We play her all the time."

"Big Maybelle," Omar said, and he remembered that early in his
career John Coltrane had worked in a band that backed Big Maybelle. Possibly, Coltrane had been playing in the music they'd just
heard. Somewhere behind that big voice, embedded in the horns,
the young Coltrane had blown a sweet tune that Omar and Carrie
had danced to; he'd played it for them, far down the corridor of time.
He had played then, as later, in the faith that this phrase, this rich
blue note, would quaver and rise and exist forever just above time,
touching down now and then to strike a tone, a moment, that married time to faith until the end of time.

"Last call," said the woman behind the bar.

He looked at Carrie. She said, "Let's do two more shooters."

Omar nodded at the bartender and watched Carrie drink her
beer.

Even as they stood there, the brief knowledge of her body, the undeniable sympathy still on his flesh, had begun to fade. Like the experience of summer, it could not be held in memory. And he wondered if, rather than Carrie or any person, it was the dream of summer he loved and would always love, the mythical season in which all things good would unfold and possess him, the summer that never quite arrived.

Gazing down the bar at the emptying tables, it came to him that actors and movies, all the machinery of illusion, existed to reproduce, however inadequately, that dream of summer. Humans needed that illusion to sustain them through the long, barren winter that their civilization had become. Carrie might even defend her vocation by declaring that his own dream of summer was a kind of Hollywood he carried in his heart.

"I wonder what became of Irma," she said. "I thought for sure we'd run into her."

He stood beside her, their elbows almost touching on the bar, and tried to hold the physical sensation of her. It was like trying to hold the memory of summer at the precise instant it hinged into fall; it occurred to him that he'd been trying to articulate that moment in his prose – the moment, dense with unnameable completion and loss, that Coltrane had captured in his ballads, the moment of lush life become the threshold for a love supreme.

The young woman placed the shot glasses on the bar.

"Did you save enough beer?" Carrie asked him. "Good. Here's how."

They touched glasses and downed the tequila.

Omar blinked and shuddered. Carrie laughed.

"Somebody told me I'm turning into an alcoholic. But I told him it doesn't change me. I mean, no matter how much I drink, I never get drunk. He said it's a matter of quantity, that anyone who drinks as much as I do is technically an alcoholic."

Omar finished his beer. "You seem to hold it pretty well," he said. "Better than me."

She turned Omar's wrist to check his watch.

"I can't believe it's that late. You can walk me home."

φ

Outside, the crowds had vanished. City workers with brooms and shovels cleaned litter from the sidewalks. The streetcars were running again, and a few stragglers stood in the middle of the street hailing taxis. Omar and Carrie walked slowly toward home.

"What will you do tomorrow?" she asked.

He thought about tomorrow and watched the taxis speeding into the night. "Work on my book, I guess. Who knows, tomorrow might be the day I finish. I might just put down my pen and say, 'That's it'."

"I'm supposed to go out on a guy's boat. Do you sail?"

"About as often as I dance."

They turned, leaving the hazy light of the broader avenue for the stranger and darker silence of their street.

"Do you like it here?" she asked. "Do you like living on this street?"

"I think it saved my life," he said.

She stared ahead. "Sooner or later I'll get my own place. I can't stay here forever."

He almost told her that she'd never leave that house. It was too late. She might try living with some man, or in an apartment in the neighbourhood, but he doubted it. And if she did, she'd come back. Omar thought that his knowing this, accepting it about her as a fact, might make him someone she could know forever. Then again, perhaps he had it all wrong. Maybe, in the fall, she'd move out. Would he still love this street if she did?

A few houses before hers, she stopped and pointed up.

"A bat!" she said, genuinely delighted. "What a good omen! There aren't enough bats in this city."

Omar looked up at the street lamp and sighted the tiny, flitting creature.

"I hadn't heard that," he said. "I hadn't heard there was a shortage of bats."

"It's true. We need more of them. They're critical to the general ecology of the city. I've never seen one before on our street."

Her voice was so girlishly sincere, so different, again, from her usual tone of complaint, he had to look at her to be sure she wasn't acting.

They sat beside each other on the low concrete wall that shored up the neighbour's lawn and watched the bat dip and whirl around the light.

"Sometimes I think I'll quit acting and go back to school in zoology. The purity of animals appeals to me. At least, the purity of studying them."

Omar shook his head. "You couldn't do it. The idea of purity appeals to you, but you're addicted to the impurities of everything else."

He felt her surprised eyes on him as he pretended to watch the bat. But she wasn't angry, and she shifted her stare back to the street lamp. The bat swooped around it and vanished in the massive darkness of treetops.

Carrie said, "I guess acting is my real vocation. Second nature, or something. My father acted. Actors hung around our house. I guess it's what I'll always do. But sometimes I feel like time is running out."

For a long minute neither of them spoke. Somewhere down the street wind chimes tinkled briefly, then stopped, as if to signal the beginning or end of a dream.

She asked him: "What year were you born?"

He glanced at her, surprised. "1957. Why?"

She nodded sagely. "I thought so."

Then she stood up and he followed her to the steps of her sidewalk, and again he stared at the names of her nephew and niece inscribed at his feet.

"Goodnight, Omar," she said, and for the second time in their acquaintance she leaned quickly to kiss his cheek.

He put his hand on her wrist and she looked at it – sadly, he thought.

"Tomorrow's another day," she said, disengaging, stepping back.

"No, it's not," he answered, having no idea what either of them had meant.

She went up the steps and hesitated. Sam the cat came tinkling out of the dark like the vanilla ghost of a cat, like the spirit of the house come to bless them, to give them one more moment.

"Sam boy!" she said, reaching down to stroke him. The cat flopped on the warm sidewalk and rolled on his back, his collar bell clinking.

As suddenly as he appeared, the cat tightened in a ball and streaked into the shadows again. Carrie straightened and watched him vanish.

"Well, goodnight," she said, taking a step toward her house. "It's nice that we're neighbours. I like to think that you're down there." She laughed. "There's something similar about us, like we're related. It's not obvious, but I feel like we're from the same tribe."

God, Omar thought. Can there be any truth in that?

As she was about to turn, he said, "I guess we don't really know each other very well. It feels like we do, but I guess we don't really have the facts."

"I got the feeling you didn't want the facts."

He stared up at the trees where the bat had vanished.

"I did though," he said. "Believe it or not, I really did."

A clear sky held a three-quarter moon that shone through a gap in the trees. He tried to remember the name for such a moon.

"Well, goodnight," she said again. "Someday we'll play tennis or something."

"Let me know," he said, and she went up to the porch and disappeared inside. A moment later the porch light winked out.

He walked home, into the deeper, but somehow altered, silence of his life on this street.

He entered his apartment without switching on lights and felt his way to the deck off the bedroom. He stood where he'd watched the fireworks hours earlier, then turned in the direction of Carrie's house. The wide northern sky held crisscrossing spotlights and blinking airplanes and one piercingly bright planet that shone steadily, almost unnaturally, where the blue distance met the black horizon. He'd had lots to drink, but he felt capable and alert; he thought he might even sit down and work for a few hours before daylight. But standing there all he knew of his precious wonder flowed toward Carrie and the shape of her life, then outward again into the world. And the world he beheld was her world, a city of summer decks extending endlessly across the luminous ether – each deck a small plateau of civilization, of charm and grace and something like revelation under the huge, blue dome of night. It was a city layered in the air, just beyond him, between the dark and mysterious earth and the hard, shining heaven. And he saw that this city was pure fancy and utterly real, like her longing to study animals, a dream of dreams fraught with actual characters and living scenes, and for the briefest moment he was on that higher deck with Carrie and Paulette and sympathetic others. There were cool drinks in their hands, citronella candles flickering at their feet and among the wine bottles on the round table. He had something to tell Carrie, but Sam the cat appeared on the railing like a small sphinx in silhouette; a child in her nightshirt stepped barefoot into the candlelight to be comforted, petted and gently returned to bed. A man spoke. A woman laughed. Carrie, glass in hand, noted the presence of the bright planet that had been shining like a god all summer. And Omar stood in that summer moment, a little apart from the others, but waiting and listening, gazing out at the vast blue wonder. Then he remembered his book was nearly finished, and he still didn't know how it would end.